ALWAYS LOOK FOR THE MAGIC
by
Bonnie Manning Anderson

Published by Prevail Press

Cover and graphic design by Anna Kester of AK Studio

Printed in the United States of America

First Printing: February 2018

ISBN - 978-09793251-7-5

D0912453

Always Look for the Magic

by

Bonnie Manning Anderson

For June & Rogan,
Hope you enjoy your read
about life in Baltimore. Be
happy!   Bonnie M Anderson

Dedicated to:

…my mom and dad, for a lifetime of loving, sharing and caring

…and to Bob, we can talk about something else now.

CHAPTER 1

June 1934 – A Magician is Born

"Hey, Tommy," I shouted as I leaned over his face. "Wake up. It's summer vacation."

"Go away, Artie. Leave me alone and be quiet before Sister Baby hears you," Tommy whispered.

Bam! The door flew open and Sister Baby appeared, all three feet of her, still in her nightgown and carrying a teddy bear by one hand. "Good morning sleepy heads! Mom says breakfast is ready. Last one down stairs is a rotten egg," she giggled and ran down the hall.

Tommy propped himself up on one elbow and asked, "What are you all energetic about? I'm usually dragging you out of bed."

"Remember Miss Spencer called me to her desk when school let out yesterday? In a million years, you'll never guess why."

"I'm guessing she wanted to give you one last note for Dad telling him your latest screw-up."

"Ha-ha. Nothing like that. She gave me a present. It's a hat."

"That's strange."

"Not strange – amazing. You know why? 'Cause the hat is… are you ready for this? Magic. The hat is magic."

"In your dreams, Artie."

"No, for real," I said as I pulled it out of the closet.

"Sounds like maybe you're the teacher's pet."

"You can call me whatever you want. I have a hat now, so I'm practically a magician," I said as I ran my hand along the brim admiring the soft black felt. The inside was smooth from wear. Though I couldn't find one secret pocket or anything that would indicate it was magic, I knew it was. It had to be.

"Why did she give it to you?" Tommy asked.

"Do you remember that essay we wrote about what we want to be when we grow up?"

"Yeah," replied Tommy. "You wanted to be a magician. I wanted to be a drummer. How come she didn't give me a set of drums?"

"Who knows? I guess you can't fit one of those in a desk drawer – that's where she found the hat, stuck in the back of a drawer. She didn't know how it got there, but she thought I could use it in my act."

"Really, she used the words 'your act?'"

"Okay, she said she thought I'd like it. Hey, maybe you can put on a dress and be my Lovely Assistant?"

Tommy's face and rolled up fist told me right away that I shouldn't joke about that, so we ran downstairs, ate breakfast and went outside to work on chopping up some downed trees for our dad. We stacked the wood to cure for winter.

Tommy was my best friend as well as my little brother. Sometimes I thought he was smarter than I was, but since he was only 10 and I was going to be 12 in four months, I could never let him know that.

We put our heads together and started to make plans. "Ever thought about sawing a woman in half?" asked Tommy.

"I thought about sawing the teacher in half every time I got a note to bring home to Dad. But I can't figure out how to do it without having a big mess to clean up."

"And then there's the putting her back together," said Tommy. "Not to mention you could end up killing somebody."

"Nah, they don't use real people. I think they use dummies like we see in store windows or like Mom's dress dummy. But hers doesn't have a head or arms, and the legs only go down to the knees. It looks like someone has already been sawing on it."

We finished stacking our wood and an idea popped into my head. I grabbed Tommy by the arm and ran back to the house. "Hey, Mom, can we go to town with you today?"

Mother looked at us with one eyebrow raised and said, "You want to go to town with me? Well, I do have to go to the butcher and the dry goods store. I'd be happy to have you along. You can carry my packages and help keep an eye on Louise."

Tommy and I shot a look at each other. We hadn't figured Louise into the equation. Louise, or Sister Baby, as we called her, was named after our mother, which made her name seem way too big for the pesky little girl that she was. The problem with her was since she was little, she couldn't keep up with us, plus she was a girl. But she was our sister, so we tried to take care of her – when we had to.

"What do you want us to do – push her in her buggy or something?" Tommy asked.

"Oh, heavens no," Mother said, "She hasn't fit into her perambulator for a couple of years. How old do you think she is anyway?"

"I don't know, three? It's hard to keep track," I offered.

"Three! She is five years old," Mother said with that frustrated tone of voice that indicated we've had this conversation before.

"We'll help with her. We'll take care of Sister Baby for you," said Tommy.

Louise, being six years younger than me, always seemed like a baby. Mother had to remind us that she would be starting school next year and her nickname of Sister Baby would have to be changed. "If you don't want to call her Louise, call her Sister."

It was settled, and the three of us kids went with Mother. She even sneaked us boys each a nickel so we could go to the drug store and buy candy. Candy was a special treat for us, and for a minute it made us forget about our plan of finding a dummy. Sister wasn't allowed in the drugstore or to have candy as somehow it made her into what Mother called "The Wild Child."

Tommy and I quickly got out of watching Sister. We ran down the street with our mouths watering for a sugary treat and left Mother shaking her head and holding Sister's hand.

The drug store had lots of candy. You could get two pieces for a nickel. Tommy pointed to the jawbreakers. "I'll bet chomping on these will help us think."

Jawbreakers last a long time. If Tommy got one, I would, too; because I can't stand for him to have his candy longer than I have mine. "Okay, we'll have two each," I told the clerk. "That'll give us one for now and one for tomorrow."

As we shuffled down the street, we tried to work out a plan, but it was difficult. I had no idea what Tommy was saying as the giant candy bulging from the side of his mouth made all his words come out garbled and the drool sliding down his chin didn't help either. Suddenly I didn't even hear the mumbled words coming from Tommy. I stopped in my tracks, mesmerized by what I saw in a store window.

"Wow," I exclaimed. "That's what we need. She looks so real."

Before we realized what we were doing, we were in the store staring at her. She was perfect and even had legs that went all the way down with feet on the end of them.

"What are you two boys doing in here?" a gruff voice from the back of the store asked accusingly. "There's nothing in here for you."

"Uh, we're trying to get a present for our mom," I lied.

"Well," he said with a noticeable change of tone, "come right in. I'm Mr. Walter. How can I help you?"

Now, two boys with no money usually won't last long in a store, but we were two boys with no money and a dream.

"Sir, our mom likes to make dresses, and she could use a new dress dummy, and we really want to get her one, and we don't have any money, but we can work for it," I said all in one breath.

"You have no idea what you're asking. These dummies are expensive, and you could work all summer and not work enough for the trade," Mr. Walter said.

We stared at him with our most pathetic faces. Finally, I said, "Please, sir, help us get a nice present for our mom."

Our disappointed faces must have struck a sympathetic nerve with Mr. Walter, because he stared down at us and then said, "Come on back to the storage room and let's see what we can do."

The storage room was a mess, but as we looked around, our hearts took a leap. There she was, leaning against the corner wall, her arms hung funny and her neck twisted like a pretzel. "This is Maggie," he said. "She has been in the store window for years and I retired her last month."

Tommy and I glanced at each other. Maggie looked like she

9

had taken quite a beating over the years. She only had one hand and her nose was flattened like she had been in a fistfight, but to us she was beautiful.

"Maggie's scheduled to go out in the garbage along with a bunch of other junk," Mr. Walter explained, "but she could be yours if you'll clean out this storage room. How's that sound for a trade? Get back here at 9:30 tomorrow morning and you can get started."

"Yes, sir," we said almost in unison. "See you tomorrow morning!"

As soon as we were outside, I said to Tommy, "What a find! I've never been so excited to clean anything in my life. Summer is starting off great."

That night when Tommy and I went to bed we could hardly sleep. We were planning all the things we could do with Maggie.

The next morning, we woke up bright and early, finished our chores and went to town. We worked hard sweeping and mopping and boxing up trash. There were shelves to fix and all kinds of sewing notions to organize. Every time we thought we were finished Mr. Walter would yell back, "Don't forget to fold up all that cardboard" or "Clean out behind those bins in the corner." I'm not sure if the place was clean enough or if he was sick of having us around, but by 3:30 we were on our way home, all three of us – Me, Tommy and Maggie.

At dinner, we told our parents about my plan to be a magician. We even told them about the magician's hat and Maggie.

"So," began Father, "you worked all day cleaning and organizing the backroom of the store."

"Yes, sir."

"You traded your sweat for a dress dummy."

"Yes, like you always say, nothing in life is free. Mr. Walter, he's the owner, said it must be our lucky day and he worked out the trade right there and then," Tommy said.

"You two are shrewd businessmen," said Father.

"There was nothing to it. Maggie's worth it for sure," I said.

"Oh, for sure. Maggie certainly is worth it. You traded your day's sweat and you got yourself Mr. Walter's trash. Yeah, you two are pretty shrewd all right. A dummy for my dummies."

"It was an honest day's work," Mother said as she looked at our dejected faces as Father left the table.

"We did get Maggie," Tommy added.

"Yeah, but we must be the two biggest idiots Mr. Walter has ever seen," I said.

"I wouldn't say that," yelled Father from the other room, "you're not that big."

CHAPTER 2

Bacon and Eggs

The next day we were up early. We finished our chores in record time and were ready to begin magic training. Our family had a shed at the top of the hill near the edge of our yard. The hill came to an abrupt stop and dropped off like a cliff onto a street below. It was the perfect place to learn the tricks of the trade. Mother almost never went up there and even Louise didn't find much to lure her in that direction.

Tommy and I carried Maggie up the hill and leaned her against the shed.

"Sawing a woman in half will make a name for us. We'll be famous the world over."

"We'll be famous alright," said Tommy. "We'll have our picture in every post office on the East Coast."

"You'll see, Tommy. I'll be the Amazing Arturo and you'll be... you'll be my manager and props guy."

13

"Thanks a lot. I guess I'll forget about the drums. Who wouldn't want to be your slave?"

"That's manager, Tommy. And you know you're in. We're a team."

"I know. I know. Grab those saw horses and let's get started."

Our father's saw horses and six two-by-fours made a great platform for our big trick. Maggie rested uncomfortably atop with a nervous look in her eyes. We got out the saw and tried to figure out how to cut Maggie in half and still be able to put her back together again. We must have walked around that platform fifty times, scratching our heads all the way.

"Do it," yelled Tommy. "Pick up the saw."

"I can't. What if we can't put her back together?"

"For crying out loud, Artie, are you going to do it or not?"

Louise came running up the hill toward us. Our crazy dog Butch, barking all the way, ran right by her side.

"Get out of here, and take that stupid dog with you," I yelled.

But Louise was unstoppable. She and Butch never slowed down. She ended up tripping over him and knocking into our platform. The two-by-fours separated, and poor Maggie went rolling over the cliff. She picked up speed, too. Louise freaked out and screamed at the top of her lungs, which made Butch bark all the more. They stood there at the edge of our cliff screaming and barking and being a complete pain in the neck.

Tommy and I took off after Maggie. I couldn't help but notice how alive she looked. We were running after her when all the sudden a truck full of chickens came around the bend. I guess the driver must have thought she looked like a live person, too, because he swerved like crazy to miss her.

He blew his horn and slammed on his brakes. His brakes squealed as he slid off of the street right into a pigpen. The pigs started squealing and escaped from their pen. The driver emerging from his truck didn't look hurt but he sure looked mad. Chickens and pigs and mud were everywhere.

"My chickens, my chickens," he shouted. Then he turned toward us, "You, you boys, I'm going to wring your little necks."

He was heading right for us, but his large form had trouble maneuvering through the mud. He grabbed a chicken and stuck it under his arm as he tried to come closer to us, but he couldn't get us and save his chickens. He shook his fist and then picked up another hen.

"Where is she? Where's Maggie?" I yelled.

"Here – she's here. Under a pile of mud," Tommy answered.

Poor Maggie looked like she had been tarred and feathered. We pulled her out of the mud as fast as we could and ran home to the sound of chickens clucking and the driver swearing. Louise was waiting for us, still screaming. I grabbed her by the shoulders and gave her my sternest look. "Shut up, Sister. Shut up. Look at me. This never happened. Do you hear me? This never happened. Now get out of here."

She instantly stopped screaming, put her hands on her hips, stuck out her tongue and skipped off singing, "Somebody's getting in trouble."

I knew my threats were useless. Even if by some miracle, Sister didn't tell on us, living in a small town like Ferndale meant you didn't have any secrets. There was no way of hiding that we were to blame for all those pigs and chickens.

Later that night a knock came on the door and two large men with one big complaint entered our living room. After each recounted to our parents the damage to his livelihood, they owned Tommy and me for the next week.

We had to wash and polish the chicken truck and clean out the mess from the back of it. Chickens really let loose when they are scared. Chicken poop smells worse than the pigs. We also had to shovel mud from the street and rebuild the pigpen, which was hard work in the heat of summer.

The pigpen was the biggest job. The pigs' trough had also been totally destroyed in the accident, so we had to build a new one. We dug holes and placed posts, and the whole time we had to make sure to keep an eye on the pigs, as they are regular escape artists. The little ones kept getting out of their temporary pen.

"You know, this experience might come in handy one day," I told Tommy.

"If you want to be a professional pigpen builder, then maybe, but right now all I see is a lot of wasted time."

"I know. Time that we could have been working with Maggie," I said as I hammered the last piece of wood for the trough. "Abracadabra. Abracadabra."

"What are you doing?"

"I'm trying to use magic to put the finishing touches on this pigpen so we can get out of here."

Tommy shook his head and said, "We have the rest of the summer. Did you get Maggie cleaned up yet?"

"Sort of. I have bad news. Her hand is missing. I looked for it, but didn't want to spend too much extra time around here, if you know what I mean."

"Today's our last day as slaves; we'll look for it on our way home."

Tommy and I split up as we climbed the hill home and sure enough, Tommy found Maggie's hand and tossed it to me.

Tommy's throw was right on and I made the catch easily. "Got it. I have her hand," I exclaimed.

My timing, however, was its usual bad. As I yelled out, a

bunch of guys walked by and gave us the business about holding Maggie's hand. It seems all the neighborhood kids found out about Maggie, so we were constantly asked how our girlfriend was.

Today I wasn't going to let it get me down. We had finished the work on the pigpen; and we were happy, though we smelled like pigs and it was weeks before we could enjoy a fried chicken dinner. To top the whole thing off, Dad liked to refer to this as the bacon and eggs incident and laughed and laughed at his clever pun, the humor of which was lost on us.

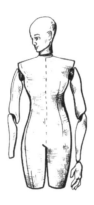

CHAPTER 3

Rabbit Hunt

I thought it was time to bring a new person into the team, and Pauline from across the street was the likeliest choice. It was important not to let the rest of the summer go by without making some strides in my quest to be a magician. We met back up by the shed – Tommy, Pauline, Maggie and me.

"First things first," I said as I put my arm around Maggie. "Pauline, this is Maggie."

"I know. The whole neighborhood knows, and how many times do I have to remind you to call me Paul?"

"Sorry, Paul, don't get your knickers in a bunch," I said mockingly. "Anyway, I know everybody thinks it's some kind of a joke that I want to be a magician, but I'm serious about it. Maggie here is going to be my greatest trick."

"Why don't you like to be called Pauline?" asked Tommy.

"I'm named after my mom's friend who is so prim and

proper I don't think she even sweats. The name doesn't seem to fit me."

"But, Paul is a boy's name," Tommy said.

"Sort of, I mean of course it is. But I wanted a shorter name and Paul works."

"And you are a tomboy."

"I guess you could say that, but I like girly stuff like dance class as much as I like to play baseball or go fishing. Let's not get all hung up about it."

"Okay, we all understand why you like to be called Paul. Now, can we get back to Maggie and working on my magic trick please, or do you two want to go off and have a cup of tea together?"

"Shut up," said Tommy.

Paul ran her finger down Maggie's dirty arm, "I thought you said you cleaned her up. She's a muddy mess and she stinks, too. The only trick I need to work on here is the one where I breathe through my mouth and keep my breakfast down. Is that the kind of magic you're talking about?"

"Very funny. Maggie has been through a lot," I continued.

"Maggie, nothing, we've lost a whole week of our summer because of her," Tommy interrupted.

"It wasn't her fault. It was Sister and that stupid dog. If she'd learn to listen none of this would have happened," I said as I peered over the cliff.

"What are you looking at?" asked Paul.

"Nothing; it's just that, we did a pretty good job down there. That's a fine-looking pigpen and the trough turned out good, too. I guess you heard about what happened."

"The whole neighborhood heard. You guys are famous. So, are you thinking about starting a pigpen business?"

"No, but Mr. Swanson, he's the guy who owns the pigs, said we could have the leftover pieces of wood if we wanted them. He was pretty nice about it. Let's go get some supplies. I have an idea."

"I don't like the sound of this at all," said Tommy as he and Paul followed me blindly down to the pig farm.

As we slid down the hill, I asked, "What is it that every magician needs?"

Paul quickly answered, "Talent?"

"Very funny, but seriously, he needs props. We have Maggie, and so far, she hasn't been too helpful."

"We also have your hat," Tommy said.

"Precisely. And when you have a hat, what do you need?"

"Tell us for Pete's sake."

"Okay, you need something to pull out of the hat. We need a rabbit."

"You're going to make one out of the wood scraps?" asked Tommy.

Paul giggled.

"Are you that stupid or are you making this way harder than it needs to be? We're going to build a trap and catch ourselves a rabbit. There are rabbits all over the place. Mom is constantly complaining about how they eat up her garden. All we have to do is trap one."

We picked up the left-over wood, a handful of nails and a piece of rope from Mr. Swanson and climbed back up the hill to make a trap.

"This is going to be a cinch," I exclaimed.

It was a little tougher than I thought it would be since our wood wasn't precisely measured, but we managed to put the thing together. Paul was pretty good with a hammer, for a girl.

Of course, I'd never say that out loud.

"You need some kind of door to swing down," Paul said. "Here, use this nail for a hinge."

"Perfect. We can tie a piece of my string to the door to pull it closed when the rabbit goes in."

"Looks great," Tommy said as we all stepped back and admired our masterpiece.

"What are you going to do with the leftovers and that piece of rope?" Paul asked.

"We'll throw those in the scrap pile and I'll hold on to the rope. I'll need to learn rope tricks, you know," I said as I pulled my other rope out of my pocket and folded them together. "We have to gather supplies wherever we can... Tommy, I don't think we should tell Mom and Dad our plan. I don't want to hear Dad tell us over and over how dumb it is."

"They're going to figure it out when they see the rabbit. Then we won't look so stupid."

"Yeah, but we'll wait until then. It'll be better that way."

Every night for six nights in a row we sneaked a few vegetables off of our plates to use as bait for the rabbits. Every night for six nights, right before dark, we ran outside to play. Our parents never thought twice about it.

The trap was easy enough to hide in the daytime up in the shed. At night we set it up in the garden area and took cover. We never had a night go by when we didn't see rabbits, but it was as if there was a sign over our trap that said, "No Rabbits Allowed." They would hop near it, over it, and around it – everywhere but in it. One particularly annoying bunny even hopped on top of it and sat there licking his paws. It was clear this wasn't going to work.

"Artie, Tommy, time to come in," called Mother. "Where are you two? Land sakes, it's almost ten o'clock."

She was coming right towards us. "Right here, Mom," I said. "I'm coming, but I think Tommy's already gone in."

Tommy looked at me with that look that bordered on confusion and anger as I held him to the ground with one foot. "Stash the trap and sneak inside," I whispered out of the corner of my mouth.

Mother turned around and I ran to walk with her. "I didn't even notice him come in," she said.

While I had Mom look for a pretend splinter in my finger, Tommy slipped upstairs without notice. Then he moseyed down the steps like nothing unusual was going on, except he was breathing awfully fast and his cheeks were bright red. He gave me the thumbs up as Mom was saying she didn't see anything at all and I probably poked it on a thorn or something.

Later that night after we went to bed I asked Tommy if he stashed the trap.

"Stash the trap? Is that what you were saying? I thought you said to set the trap. It was hard to hear you with your foot planted on my back and my head in the dirt. We'll have to get it in the morning."

That was going to be a challenge as our parents were always up before us. But the next morning I managed to get up, go outside and move the trap out of view before our secret was uncovered.

Paul came over, and the three of us began putting our heads together.

"I think the rabbits are too smart for you," Paul said. "We need to move that trap farther away from the house."

"Yeah, and we need some kind of a trip wire on it so it can close without us being around," said Tommy.

We rigged up a wire to close the door when a bunny entered the box and set it every night before we went in at dark. We used carrots from Mom's garden as the lure as we figured out rabbits don't like cooked food as much as they do raw. On the third morning of our new procedure Tommy and I ran out to the trap and something was definitely inside.

"I can't believe it," Tommy yelled.

"Pipe down. You want to wake the whole neighborhood?"

"Sorry. Let's have a look. Open it up."

"Not so fast," I said as I circled the trap a time or two. "Dad's right. We are stupid sometimes. We didn't think about where we were going to put a rabbit if we caught one. We can't keep it in this trap forever. Here, Tommy, you sit on it and keep it shut while I figure things out."

I ran back to the house with my mind blank as slate. I barely noticed Sister sitting on the step. "What ya doing?" she asked.

"Nothing. Get lost," I answered as I ran by.

Getting lost was not part of Louise's plan that morning. She followed me around the house like a hungry puppy, only she wasn't cute like a puppy. She was just plain annoying. She sang her little songs and talked without stopping and even followed me into my room.

Finally, she yelled down to Mother, "Mother, make Artie play with me."

"Not now, Louise, you haven't done you chores."

I stuck my tongue out at her, grabbed my pillow, pulled the case off of it and ran out as fast as I could.

Meanwhile, poor Tommy was sitting on top of our prize and waiting not-so patiently. What else could he do? At least Paul had shown up and was keeping him company.

"This thing is making some pretty weird noises. What took you so long?"

"Sister – that's what took me so long. Okay, now do you want to be the rabbit-grabber or the trap-opener?"

After much discussion on the pros and cons and dangers of handling a wild rabbit, we decided that I should bag the rabbit. Quickly Tommy pulled the door open as I covered the opening with my pillowcase. I expected the rabbit to hop right in but nothing happened. Then something slowly crept into the pillowcase.

We looked at each other. Tommy was jumping up and down like he was about to pee his pants.

"Presto! We got a big one," I yelled. "We are amazing." I held our prize out to my side in triumph. It was then that we heard something puzzling.

Paul was first to figure it out, "I don't know if you heard what I did, but I've never heard a rabbit make a sound like that."

"What sound does a rabbit make?" I asked.

"I don't know that they make any sound, so unless we hear nothing, we probably don't have a rabbit in there," Paul said.

"That's ridiculous. Hearing nothing doesn't mean anything. It could mean we have something dead in there," I said.

"Like maybe a dead rabbit," Tommy offered.

"You guys are hopeless. Dead things don't crawl into a bag. Open it," Paul said.

Triumph turned quickly to disappointment when we opened the pillowcase and saw our cat.

That night we decided we might as well bite the bullet and tell Dad what we'd been up to. "Dad, have you noticed that Tommy and I have been spending a lot of time outside at night?"

"That's not unusual, Artie. You guys practically live out there in the summer."

"Well, we've been doing some trapping. Some rabbit trapping."

"Rabbits? Catch any?"

"Nah, we almost did. Our stupid cat got himself caught in the trap, but we're not giving up."

"Not giving up is a good thing, I suppose, but it seems like this is a colossal waste of time. But, since you're kids and it's summertime, I reckon you have some time to waste. Check in the shed for some more scraps and make yourselves another trap or two. Who knows, maybe you can surround them, though I wouldn't get my hopes up. Seems pretty unlikely you'll catch anything more than a summer cold."

The next morning, we went to the shed where we found everything we needed to make two more traps. There was also an old cage stuffed back in the corner behind some rakes that Dad told us we could use, again as he put it, "in the unlikely event that you two can actually catch anything."

That made us all the more determined. We constructed our new traps and had them ready before nightfall. We took the old cage up to the house and placed it under our back steps, so it would be easy to retrieve. Another week of setting the traps at night, checking the traps in the morning, and grumbling over our inability to catch a rabbit passed. By this time, we were pretty certain we would never catch a rabbit, just like our dad had predicted. I was no closer to being a magician. Maggie wasn't working out, and now rabbits seemed to hate me.

At least it was summer. The neighborhood kids congregated nightly and even parents came outside. They would stand around sipping their lemonade and iced tea and we kids would play tag or hide and seek.

The adults didn't seem like they were having the good time that we were. I didn't think much of it at first; but one night while I was "frozen" during freeze tag, I overheard one man say that he had lost his job and another comment that his wasn't looking too good either. I even heard our own father tell them that he wasn't sure how he was going to keep food on the table. Then Paul ran by and unfroze me and I was off again.

At bedtime, I asked our mother, "Are we poor?"

"I guess I never thought about labeling us as something, but if we had to, poor wouldn't be much of an exaggeration these days," she said as she turned out the light.

"Mom… Mom, what's for breakfast tomorrow?" I yelled to her.

"Cereal and toast," she replied, "now get some sleep."

"What do you care about breakfast now?" Tommy asked.

"Just wondering…" I decided it wouldn't be a good idea to let Tommy know that, not only were we poor, but we might be coming up on poor and hungry.

Almost immediately our room filled with the sound of Tommy's deep breathing as he fell asleep, but I couldn't stop thinking about what I heard. I sneaked to the top of the stairs and stood there. The house was quiet except for the disturbing sound of my mother crying in her room.

Sure enough, the next morning we had cereal and toast for breakfast. Mom was up as usual and seemed pretty happy as she hummed a tune while washing out the coffee pot. Maybe I heard wrong. Maybe everything was fine. I couldn't stop thinking about it, until suddenly I realized that Mom was talking to me.

"Well, Artie, aren't you going to take a guess?"

I sat there blankly trying to catch up with the conversation.

Sister said, "I'll take his guess. I guess we're having cake for dinner."

"That's a guess of cake and a guess of pie from Louise, and

a guess of mashed potatoes from Tommy. How about you, Artie, what do you think our special dinner will be?"

"Oh, I don't know. Liver and onions?"

A collective "ugh" went up from Tommy and Sister. Mom laughed. "You'll have to wait and see. Now finish up your breakfast and get to your chores. You boys slept in quite a bit after all that running around last night. Remember your dad is picking you up later this morning so you can help him at the bakery."

It was yard day – the most hated day of the week. To make it worse Dad wanted our help down at the bakery. Our chore was mowing the grass and weeding. The mower was hard to push and weeding wasn't much better. It was Tommy's turn to mow and my turn to weed.

I went out to the garden with my basket for the weeds, hating our chores. I had forgotten about checking the trap that was placed at the edge of the garden today. When I saw the trap door was closed, my heart beat hard in my chest; but as I tapped it with my foot, it was clear there was no rabbit inside.

Down on my knees weeding, all I could think about was that summer was flying by and we didn't have a rabbit. If we didn't catch one before the end of summer, the rabbits will go wherever it is that they go when fall comes, and I'll have to wait another year. With every weed that I pulled I was getting madder until I got up, ran over to the trap and kicked it as hard as I could. This turned out to be a stupid thing to do with bare feet, the fact to which my foot immediately testified.

I grabbed my foot and hopped around the garden, the pain bringing a new level of anger at myself and my situation. My foot was red and ached like the dickens. I hobbled over to the back step to examine it. The toes all wiggled, though not without pain; and the entire instep of my foot was going from red to purple in a hurry. I stood up to test how it felt with my weight on it, and Tommy came over to check on me.

"I think I'm okay. I'm just an idiot."

It was then that we heard it – a soft sound from under the steps. We both cocked our heads to one side like hunting dogs would, and then we peeked under the steps.

"It's a rabbit!" I exclaimed, forgetting all about my throbbing foot. "A perfect brown and white rabbit."

Tommy asked, "How'd it get in the cage?"

"It's a miracle," I said. "A miracle. We'll name him Ralph – Ralph the Rabbit."

We happily went back to our chores and finished them as our father pulled up and announced we needed to get a move on. We dropped everything and piled in the bakery truck with him.

"Well," he asked, "did you see it?"

"The rabbit? Yes, sir. How'd it get in there?"

Father replied, "I was up very early and noticed one of your traps acting funny. I figured I better get that rabbit out of there and into the cage before it escaped."

"Oh man, that's great. I can't wait to see how he works out in my hat."

After a full day of cleaning and organizing at the bakery, Father said we were finished working. He locked up and the three of us went home.

I was pretty hungry and that made my father's words about putting food on the table flow through my brain again. When we opened the front door and took in the smells of Mom's cooking, those words disappeared like the steam escaping from the large pot on the table.

"You're right on-time. Now wash up and sit down for supper," said Mother.

When we got to the table, Mother and Sister were already

there. Mom picked right up from our breakfast conversation. "Well, nobody guessed what the surprise dinner would be. It's stew," she said as she ladled some into Father's bowl.

After everyone was served, Father said the blessing and we all started eating. Then he said, "There's meat in this stew, Louise. Where did you get the meat?"

"Come now, Arthur; you know exactly where I got it."

Father looked confused.

"You are a tease, Arthur. You know it's rabbit."

"Rabbit!" Tommy and I said in unison.

"Yes, when I went out to wave goodbye to you this morning, I heard a noise under the steps. When I looked, there was dinner waiting to be prepared. I figured you must have put it there for me to fix or else it was a gift from God – you know, a miracle."

My hunger was gone. I could hardly look at the stew. I put my spoon in the bowl and tried to ladle some out, but it was no use. I'd never be hungry enough to eat Ralph. I excused myself from the table and ran from the room. Tommy was right on my heels. Dad was gobbling down stew like there was no tomorrow.

"I don't think I can bring myself to keep trying to trap rabbits if Mom's going to cook them," I said.

"I'm glad she can't make anything out of Maggie or your hat," Tommy said, "or else you'd be out of business."

CHAPTER 4

The More, the Merrier

Later that night a knock came on the door and we ran downstairs to find Uncle Lyle, Aunt Catherine and our cousins, William, Bucky, Leroy and Edgar. Mother put on the coffee pot and sent us kids upstairs.

"We didn't know you were coming over, Bucky. What's up?" I asked.

"Nothing good. Dad's been out of work a long time, and I think we're getting kicked out of our house," said Bucky.

Leroy added, "I heard Mom talking about moving in with the grandparents, but Dad's not keen on it."

William said, "They've been packing stuff up for a week now. It doesn't look good."

"That sounds bad. They live way over in Baltimore. We'd never get to see you," I said.

"Yeah, like that's their biggest problem," Tommy chimed in.

"That's okay, Artie. I know what he means," said William.

"If it makes you feel any better, I think we're poor, too."

"Shut up, Artie. You don't know what you're talking about," Tommy said.

"I hear stuff, and Mom even said we're poor," I added.

Mother called from the bottom of the stairs, "Boys, Louise, come down here for a few minutes."

We lined up in the living room waiting for a speech.

"Children," Father began. "You've probably figured out that money's pretty tight. Well, it's been rough not only for us, but for Uncle Lyle and Aunt Catherine, too. Seems the best idea might be for us all to live in the same house together. What do you think about that?"

We liked it fine for the most part. Tommy and I had been sharing a room. Now we'd share a bed, and not only with each other, but there'd be a cousin or two in there with us as well.

It wasn't bad; except sometimes Edgar still peed the bed, and I'd end up sleeping on the floor shivering in wet pajamas that I didn't even wet. But, as Mother would remind us, we're family and we stick together through thick and thin, dry and wet – the more, the merrier. That was easy for her to say. She didn't have to share a bed with Edgar.

Our cousins had been living with us for less than a week when a "SOLD" sign went up on the empty warehouse at the edge of our little town. At a time when many people were out of work, the possibility of a new company setting up a business was pretty exciting.

Soon a sign appeared on the building – "The Steering Committee." Fences were constructed around the borders of the property. Trucks started arriving with supplies. "Help Wanted" signs popped up around town. Everything happened quickly.

At dinner one night, Uncle Lyle wanted to ask the blessing. "Thank you, God, for the food we're about to eat and thank you for taking care of me and my family today by finding me a job. Amen."

Aunt Catherine sprung up out her chair and hugged him.

"Oh my soul, Lyle. I was beginning to lose hope after a year of you looking. And now being put out of our home..." She started to cry.

"There, there, Catherine, wipe those tears. We may have been down but we're not out." Then he looked at the rest of us and said, "You're all going to like my new job. It's at that new place in town. It's a meat packing company and that means that now and then I might even be able to bring us home a steak for dinner."

Aunt Catherine looked so proud, and Dad and Mom seemed excited, too. But never having tasted a steak before, the excitement about it was pretty much lost on us.

Uncle Lyle explained, "When the cows arrive we try to keep them fed and calm. They say a calm cow is a tender cow."

Leroy blurted out, "You've gotta get us in there. Maybe you can show us how to rope a cow. You're going to be a regular cowboy."

"Sorry, fellas, no kids allowed anywhere near the place."

"We can't even look at the cows or pet one?" Bucky asked.

"Nope, it's no place for kids."

And that was it. It all sounded strange. Why would anybody have a bunch of cows that we weren't allowed to go see? What was so special about them?

CHAPTER 5

Cow Parade

One night Tommy, Leroy and I heard Uncle Lyle talking about the big shipment of cows that was coming in on Saturday. He was going to have to work overtime, and he was grateful for the opportunity.

We, too, were grateful for the opportunity and figured we would sneak on down to the Steering Committee and catch a look at all those cows. Maybe we could even pet one.

When we arrived, the cows were being herded from the big trucks through the gate. It was like a parade. We found a pen full of cows, and we were even able to squeeze our hands through an opening and touch one. Their eyes were big and friendly and their tongues were rough. William, Bucky, Leroy and Edgar were so proud that their dad was a cowboy.

"Hey, guys, remember we're not supposed to be here. I don't want to get in trouble. Anybody spotted your dad yet?" Tommy asked.

"You worry too much, Tommy," I said as I looked around.

"There, over there by that gate. See him?" William said.

"What's he doing with that giant hook?" Bucky asked.

We looked back at the cow parade and saw a very large man approach the cows. He had some kind of big club or something in his hand and all of the sudden he clobbered the cow on the head.

"No!" Leroy and Edgar yelled in unison.

Then Uncle Lyle guided the big hook down the rope and hooked the cow on it and slid it down the line. Another man grabbed the dead cow and started slaughtering it right in front of our eyes. It was horrible. Blood was everywhere.

"Uncle Lyle is a cow murderer," I exclaimed as Leroy doubled over and threw up.

William grabbed up Edgar, and we all ran out of there as fast as our legs would take us. Leroy was turning green and could barely stand so we half dragged him away from there.

"We have to do something. We have to save the cows," I stated like some kind of superhero.

Bucky cleaned up Leroy and the six of us made our way back to the cow pen. It took some doing, but we got the pen open.

Now, we hadn't thought this through much, and suddenly Tommy decided to take charge. He stood up on the fence and yelled, "Ye ha," over and over again.

I took off my red plaid shirt and waved it at the cows to attract them to the gate, which William and Edgar held open. Then Bucky and Leroy started smacking the cows on their backside, and before we knew it there was a full-fledged stampede running right toward town.

We didn't do a very good job of not being noticed. Instantly there were trucks trying to round up the cows and men yelling and swearing. It took two days to round up the last of them.

We got the scolding of our lives. Uncle Lyle was so upset he wouldn't talk to Tommy and me, though I heard him shouting at his sons.

Dad said, "You guys are lucky that hare-brained scheme didn't cost your uncle his job!"

Tommy said, "We're sorry. Really, we are. But, it was awful seeing those cows…"

"Awful. I'll tell you what's awful. Being out of work is awful. Wondering how you will feed your family is awful. Slaughtering a cow – that's just what needs to be done."

"We are sorry," I said. "We thought…"

"No, you didn't think. That's the problem. What would you do with a cow if you rescued one? You can't pull a solution for that out of your hat, can you Artie? Think about that for a while."

We had lots of time to think about it. We were grounded for a week.

CHAPTER 6

Take Me to Your Leader

Uncle Lyle was bringing meat home for our dinner once a week now. On Sundays, Mother and Aunt Catherine would fix biscuits, mashed potatoes and gravy, and a roast that Uncle Lyle would supply. It was our weekly feast and day of thanksgiving.

The grown-ups would sit around and talk about all kinds of stuff, like banks and who was working and who was not. We children were not allowed to talk during dinner unless we were answering a question or asking for something to be passed to us, and then we had to be very polite. It was hard, especially since Louise could get away with talking all she wanted. It drove me crazy.

It was not unusual for us to have company for dinner. Dad or Uncle Lyle often brought somebody home that needed a meal. Tonight's guest was Mr. Slack; he worked with Uncle Lyle. He had a surprise for us, which made it hard to sit still through dinner. We kids tried to guess what it was.

"A kitten?" asked Sister.

"No, not a kitten. It isn't alive."

"A magic trick?" I asked hopefully.

"I don't know any magic, but I'd say that what I have to show you is out of this world – it seems magical to me," said Mr. Slack.

When it got dark we stepped out in our backyard; and there, all set up, was a telescope. We had never seen one before.

"Neat! Do you think we can see a shooting star or an asteroid or a Martian or something like that?" I asked.

William added, "In school we learned about Hooveria Asteroid that was named after President Hoover. That would be amazing to see."

"Yeah, and how great would it be to have a planet or something named after you. Maybe we could discover a new planet and name it Manning after our last name," I said.

"Maybe someday we would find life on Planet Manning. Or, maybe one day a man could travel to Manning," Tommy said.

"Who knows, maybe" said Mr. Slack. "There was a time when we didn't have a telescope to see in space, so we can only imagine what the future will bring. It's exciting to think about."

"Yeah, sure. That'll be the day – traveling in space. I guess we'll all go have lunch on the moon," Father said with a mocking laugh.

"I don't think that is far-fetched. I can imagine it," Uncle Lyle said.

Imagining was exactly what Tommy and I were doing. We thought it would be great to meet spacemen. We pictured them as little and green with red eyes. We were sure that they were out there.

Looking through the telescope was pretty nifty all right but also a little disappointing. I guess we had pictured a pair of those bright red eyes looking back at us, but everything except the moon looked like stars. We were able to see Mars. It was sort of red and looked a little different from the other stars because of that, but it was no big deal.

The best part of the night came later when Tommy and I pretended to invade our little sister's room. We sneaked up on her and said in our best Martian voice — "We-are-from-the-planet-Mars. Take-us-to-your-leader." And it worked. Sister screamed so loudly that her leader came to us. We got in trouble, too. Waking up a sleeping earthling can be pretty hard on a visiting Martian.

All week we kept pretending to be Martians. We were obsessed. We wanted to meet a Martian, even though we were totally convinced that they would be dangerous. Any self-respecting Martian would have to take us up into his flying saucer and we might never return to Earth again. By Saturday, Mother was ready for us to go back to being magicians. "If I hear you call your sister an Earthling one more time or ask me for Martian food, so help me!"

CHAPTER 7

The Mystery of the Red Eye

"Your father may end up working late at the bakery. Why don't you two go help him and see if you can speed things along?"

We didn't mind going to the bakery on Saturday. We would have to help with the cleaning, but there were leftovers that we could eat, so it almost evened out.

"You men are just in time," Dad said as we walked in the door. He always called us men when it was time to work. We snapped to attention, and he directed us to our stations. If Dad whistled while he worked, we knew he was happy to have us with him. If we fell down on our duties, the whistling stopped abruptly. That was our signal to keep our eyes down, our noses to the grindstone, and work hard so he wouldn't holler at us. It never worked. He'd bark out some chore or show us an area that needed more attention before we could convince him we were working.

Today we had been working hard for a couple of hours when Dad said, "I'm going to have to stay late tonight. You fellows go home and see if your mother needs any help."

I thought it was interesting how each of our parents wanted us to help the other parent.

"Let's cut through the graveyard. It'll save us some time," Tommy said.

"We have plenty of time. The sun is starting to go down, but if we get home too fast Mom will make us take a bath."

"You're chicken to walk through the graveyard, afraid we'll get caught in there after dark," Tommy taunted.

"Am not."

"Are too."

"Am not!"

"Are too," Tommy shouted as he turned off the road.

The sun was going down fast, but there was a full moon rising. We figured we'd be able to see well enough, but I still had the heebie-jeebies. The trees made it even darker and, well, we were surrounded by dead people. I didn't like this place in the daytime, much less at night. I couldn't let Tommy know that, so I took a deep breath and we headed in.

It was so quiet that all we could hear was the sound of our footsteps and our breathing. It took a few minutes before we calmed down and didn't notice our breathing any more. We were about halfway through and had managed to avoid stepping on "anybody." We even started talking and planning how to scare Sister again. We were laughing and plotting when all of the sudden I felt Tommy's hand grab my arm.

"What are you doing? Let go," I said. But Tommy's death grip told me that he wasn't about to let go. When I looked at his face, his eyes were as big as saucers.

"Artie, do you see that? Over there, it's a red flashing light."

And there it was. The red glow grew stronger and then fainter. We froze in our tracks. Beads of sweat popped out on our foreheads and the hair on the back of our necks stood straight up.

"May, may, maybe it's a Martian," I whispered. "Maybe he only has one eye in the middle of his forehead. Maybe we're watching that eye blinking."

"Or worse, maybe he's watching us. Maybe he was looking at us since that night with the telescope, and now he's mad at how we've been making fun of him."

We jumped behind a headstone. Our hearts were beating so hard I think I heard them. I was breathing so loudly I was sure the Martian could hear me. "Artie, stop breathing!" Tommy forcefully whispered.

I tried holding my breath, but I ended up letting out an even louder gasp of air. We waited and waited. Nothing happened. We peeked out from behind the tombstone and could see nothing unusual.

"It's almost completely dark. We can't stay here all night. Come on. Quit being a sissy and let's head for home."

We gathered our courage and stepped out into the open. It was only minutes before we saw it again – the red, blinking eye! It was between us and home. I went to grab Tommy, but he wasn't there! I turned around to see Tommy running faster than I'd ever seen him go before.

Out of breath and scared to death, we arrived back at the bakery in time to see our father lock the door. He was surprised to see us, but before he could ask any questions, we were telling him our story. We told him all about being watched by the Martian.

"A Martian? You have quite the imaginations," Father said.

As we walked along and he turned into the graveyard, Tommy begged him, "Please don't take us through there."

"Dad, he waits until you're good inside and then he shows

up. Please don't go this way," I pleaded.

"There has to be some kind of reasonable explanation," Father said. "Come on."

We didn't need an explanation, reasonable or otherwise; we needed to get out of there. But Father couldn't be convinced, so in we went.

"Well, whatever was scaring you boys doesn't seem to be here now. I think you had a bit too much Martian play this week."

The words were barely out of his mouth when the red eye appeared. Tommy and I screamed so loudly that our father jumped and nearly fell into a marble grave marker. Normally that would have Tommy and me laughing like crazy, but not tonight.

"You boys stay right here. I'll go check this out and come back for you."

As Dad walked out of sight I said, "I don't think I ever want to be a father. They have to do all the worst jobs."

"I hope they don't take him up away from us," Tommy said. "Why couldn't we take the long way?"

"This would be a great time to have a magic wand," I whispered.

We huddled behind a grave marker for a long time. By now it was real dark and even though it was summertime we had chills running down our spines.

"He's been gone too long. Maybe it got him! What are we going to tell Mom? We have to do something," I told Tommy.

As we were about to stand up and face our fear, Dad appeared. "Come with me," he said with a serious tone.

Tommy and I looked at each other and gulped. We had no choice. We followed our father, who looked straight ahead and didn't even blink. He wouldn't answer our questions, but kept walking toward the red eye.

"It must have gotten to him, and now he's taking us to it!" I whispered.

"Please, don't take us to him. Remember Mom. Remember Sister," Tommy cried.

But he wouldn't stop. We grew closer and closer to the red eye and then, suddenly, it went out. It was dark and quiet and Dad kept on walking.

When we thought we couldn't stand it anymore, we heard a strange scratching noise, and then the eye reappeared. In a voice that sounded eerily calm and collected, our father said, "Boys, I never thought it would end like this. I didn't believe in Martians, but how else can we explain this?"

Then, as he pointed into the darkness he said, "I'll tell you how else. I'd like you to meet Clay. He's on night shift here, and this is where he sits and puffs on a cigarette, or as you boys would prefer to call it, the red-eyed Martian."

Then the two men laughed for a long time. Dad actually had tears streaming down his face from laughing so hard. Clay would puff on the cigarette and make the red end of it glow brighter, and they would laugh again. It took Tommy and me a long time before we thought it was funny.

By the time we got home, Mom had put Sister to bed and had gone to bed herself. Tommy and I were changing into our pajamas and brushing our teeth, when roars of laughter came from our parents' room. Time to go back to being a magician. Martians are too much trouble.

CHAPTER 8

Whistling in the Dark

At church, there were a lot of people asking for prayer and all the prayers were about people needing jobs and money. This Great Depression, as they called it, didn't seem great to me. To make things worse, the Steering Committee was letting people go.

As we walked home from church, Mother reminded us, "We'll see what the Good Lord has in store for us. We haven't gone hungry yet, and I'm sure He will provide everything we need. Our part is to remember that we don't need nearly as much as we think we do."

That was a statement that I wouldn't fully understand until later.

As we sat around the dinner table that night Uncle Lyle told us what was going on at the Steering Committee. "There's not a demand for beef. People are having trouble paying their bills, with the Depression dragging on. Everybody's eating soup and there's barely any beef being sold."

"What does that mean for you, Lyle?" Mother asked.

"Well, the Steering Committee is pulling out of town and

closing their doors. They haven't been able to make a profit so they are going to cut their losses. I am one of the lucky ones. I get to keep working for one more week to help close the business."

After dinner, we kids were quickly excused to go and play. We didn't even have to help clear the table. Our parents wanted to talk.

As we went upstairs, I heard Father confide to Uncle Lyle that he had exactly enough money to pay the rent for one more week, and he was worried. The whole town was feeling the strain. The bakery closed yesterday. He, too, was out of a job.

All of this was ringing in my ears as we ran to get our marbles. We grabbed our shooters and aggies and went out to play. Tommy made a line in the dirt, and we rolled for who would go first. I tried to focus in on playing, leaving the adult problems to the adults.

Bucky won the roll, much to our dismay. It was rare for Bucky to lose at lagging the line, as it was called. He was so precise in his shooting and could roll his marble within a hair's width of the line. He was the closest thing to a champion marble player our neighborhood had ever seen. He always wanted to play for keeps. That's how he ended up with the most marbles. Sometimes he would win so fast that we barely had time to play. Today we would play for fair, and all the winner would get was glory.

All our yelling attracted other kids in the neighborhood; and before we knew it, we had a tournament going on. I lost my marbles fast and was out, so I cheered on Tommy until he was out, too. Soon it was just Bucky and Leroy. Bucky ended up winning.

After all the marbles had been returned to their owners, I worked on hiding a marble under a cup. I had seen a guy with three cups and one pea do the trick of having somebody find the pea. It was amazing how hard it was to find. I figured I could do that with one of my marbles, but they roll too easily so it didn't work. It was another trick I couldn't do. How do people become magicians anyway? That itself must be magic.

It was getting dark and we heard Dad whistle for us. The entire neighborhood heard it, but we knew it was meant for us. I was working on my whistle and could do it almost as loudly as he could. Sometimes I even fooled Tommy into thinking that it was our dad calling him when it was me.

That night from our room we looked out the window and saw a taxicab going down the street. I leaned out and whistled, and it stopped. The driver got out of his car and looked around. We ducked down below the window so that he couldn't see us.

This had become our favorite game. We named it Hail a Cab. Sometimes we would hide up in a tree and whistle for a taxicab. Sometimes we would hide on somebody's roof. The trick was to keep moving, never use the same hiding place twice.

While we were laughing and talking about it, Father came up to see what we were up to.

"Nothing. We're just sitting here by the window, getting some air."

Without even the smallest hint of a smile he said, "Children, things are getting rougher. Uncle Lyle and I are both out of work. We are going to have to be extra careful with our belongings and our money." He dropped that bomb on us, turned, and left our room.

I couldn't imagine how we could be more careful. I was used to walking with cardboard in my shoes to cover holes from wear. We did not go out anywhere that cost money. I couldn't remember the last time I got a new shirt or pants. Everything was a hand-me-down from my cousins, and Tommy got my stuff. Sister was the only one who got anything new, and that was because she was the only girl. Even so, sometimes she wore our old shirts and overalls. However rough things were for us before, this Depression was making them worse.

CHAPTER 9

The Mystery of the Unanswerable Knock

In the morning, Mom came up to our room and told us all to be very quiet and stay in bed. We heard a knock on the door downstairs. Then we heard it again, but for some reason no one was answering the door. After a few minutes, Mom said, "Okay, come on down for breakfast."

This was a strange way to start the day. I didn't know if I should ask who was at the door or not. Breakfast was quiet. We ate oatmeal so you couldn't even hear a crunch. Quietly, I asked, "Who was at the door?"

"Oh," Dad said, "did someone come to the door?"

And that was it. It was a mystery.

It was a little creepy at home now. Every morning Dad would head out and look for work, but there was no work to be had. Uncle Lyle wasn't having any better luck. Mom and Aunt Catherine tried to keep the mood upbeat at home, but you could feel the tension.

Dinner was small and took no time to eat. After dinner Tommy and I went outside to find something to do. We needed to run off some energy, Mom said. After searching high and low and coming up empty, we decided to play Hail a Cab. It was going to be dark soon, so we shimmied up an oak tree and waited. Soon a cab happened by and I was up to bat.

I whistled my loudest whistle. Brakes squealed and a big, burly guy emerged from the cab. He looked around, scratched his head and crawled back into his cab. We laughed like crazy.

It was a long time before another cab passed by, and we were about to go home when we spied headlights. It was a cab! I whistled and once again brakes squealed – it was the same guy. When he looked around and didn't see anyone, he wasn't happy. Grumbling all the way, he got back inside his car and drove off.

We laughed and laughed and waited a little while longer to see if another one came by. We didn't have to wait long. My whistle pierced the quiet night and sure enough, brakes squealed again. This time the car pulled over, and out climbed the same man closing the door behind him. His arms were crossed in front of him, and I think steam might have actually been coming out of his ears.

"Don't move, Tommy!"

"Don't worry! I don't think he can see us," Tommy whispered.

"Hey, I know you're out there. I have plenty of time to wait, too," the driver yelled as he got a flashlight out of his car.

We froze our positions and hoped that the tree would hide us. It didn't.

"I guess you think you're all kind of clever making me stop for nothing," he said as he aimed the light right at us.

"We've been made," Tommy said.

"Shut up!" I said.

"Talk, don't talk. It doesn't matter to me. It'll be easy to find out where you two live. All I have to do is ask around where do two brats live and somebody will finger you."

"I'm starting to slip, Tommy. I don't know how long I can stay here."

"It better be long. He's going to kill us if he gets his hands on us."

The driver yelled, "Yep, I think you two have a good thrashing coming to you, and nobody will blame me either."

For an angry man, he was very patient. It was a contest as to who would move first. He sat at the foot of the tree and stared at us. It wasn't too hot out, but Tommy and I were sweating like pigs.

"I'm falling," I said. "My hands can't hold on much longer and besides I have to pee."

"It's your nerves, Artie. Hang on. You know we're in trouble one way or the other. We've been gone a long time so either this guy's going to kill us or Dad is."

"I'm going to try to reason with him. I can't take this anymore," I said. "Sir?"

"Yeah, you better call me sir."

"Sir, I was hoping we could work out something with you. Something that doesn't involve you beating the tar out of us."

"Interesting. How about one of you comes down and stays with me and the other one goes and gets your father? Tell him to bring a first aid kit in case I get bored waiting."

Suddenly we heard his radio click on and he was sent out on a call. "It must be your lucky night, kids. But, you can be sure I'll see you later."

When his brake lights were out of sight, we climbed down and ran home as fast as we could.

Our parents hardly noticed us come into the house. I guess everything else going on worked in our favor. We went straight to our room and told our cousins about our adventure. We laid it on thick about how we got away from this huge cab driver and how brave we were. We were in the middle of telling about the stare down when we heard a knock at the front door. In another three minutes, we were called to the living room by our full names. We swallowed hard and walked down the stairs with fear and trembling.

"Yeah, those are the little brats who kept whistling for my cab," yelled the man with the gruffest voice I had ever heard.

He was even bigger than he looked before. Dad invited him into our house and told him that he would take care of us. We were sent to our rooms to await our meeting with Dad. It took a long time for him to come up. Leroy peeked down into the kitchen and saw our father talking to the cab driver. They were having a cup of coffee and even laughing. We figured they were planning the best punishment for us.

"We're going to get killed," Tommy kept saying over and over.

"They're not going to kill us. Don't be stupid," I said.

"It's all your fault. How do you talk me into doing these things?" asked Tommy.

"You were all in and you know it."

Tommy began, "One thing I did pick up from history is that punishments are made to fit the crime. They might cut off somebody's fingers for stealing or something like that."

"You're ridiculous, Tommy. They don't do that anymore. Besides, we're kids."

"They could cut off your whistling fingers or slice your tongue out," offered Leroy. "They could."

We stared at Leroy, wondering where gruesome thoughts like that came from. I thought Tommy was going to cry, and I kept having to keep my mind from wandering down that dark path

56

and hoped to keep all ten of my fingers and my tongue, too.

Dad never came up that night. Tommy and I waited and waited and then gave in to sleep. When we woke up and realized that we had gone all night without a punishment, we were scared. Now we had two mysteries – the mystery of the unanswered knock at our door and the mystery of why we didn't get punished for hailing cabs.

Soon Mom called us for breakfast and one mystery was solved. Yes, we were in big trouble. Mr. Humphrey, the cab driver, was very angry. He had missed a fare when he turned around to find us and he said that if he didn't own the cab company, he would have fired himself. We thought that sounded funny, but when we started to chuckle, Dad got mad.

"That man is out there trying to make a living and provide for his family. You two think this is funny?"

Another trip to the woodshed – we knew we had it coming, but for some reason that didn't make it hurt any less.

CHAPTER 10

The Mystery Continues

During dinner, we heard another knock on the front door. I jumped up to answer, but Mom told me to sit down and not worry about it. Once again, the door was not being answered.

The knock came again – this time harder. Again, we all sat quietly still.

"Can I answer the door?" Sister asked.

"No," answered Dad.

I could not stand it any longer. "Why don't we answer the door?"

"Don't worry, dear," said Mom.

But we did worry. Our parents were acting very strangely. There were times when Mom would quickly call us into the house and have us take a nap and be quiet. Then in ten minutes, we could get up and she acted like nothing was unusual.

We kids decided to have a meeting. "William, Bucky, Leroy, Tommy, we have a case to solve. A detective case."

"What about Edgar and Louise?" Tommy asked.

"Let's not include them in this. They're too little."

Leroy said, "I thought you were a magician. What's this detective business?"

"We have a mystery going on and I'm out to solve it. It's driving me crazy! My magic will have to wait."

"I think it will be fine waiting," Leroy said.

William added, "That's enough, Leroy."

"This is about Mom not letting us answer the door, isn't it?" Tommy asked.

"Precisely! Now are you with me or not?"

William, Bucky, Leroy, Tommy and I set out to solve the case. We had noticed that every night after we went to bed, our parents would talk to each other in whispers. Sometimes we heard Mom or Aunt Catherine crying. We decided to spy on them.

After bedtime, Tommy sneaked down the stairs and listened in. As he told us what he heard, I thought he was going to cry. "You know all those knocks on the door?"

"Yes. Can we not do the question and answer thing please? Tell us what you heard," William said.

"Okay, sorry. Well, there were knocks. And there were people at the door that our parents were trying to avoid. They were either bill collectors or the landlord. Our families are broke!"

We never thought much about money. It didn't seem important, but we knew that if our parents didn't have any, we were all in trouble. Already some of our friends had moved away, and "for rent" signs kept going up around the neighborhood as more and more men lost their jobs.

It was only a few more mornings and another knock came as we all sat at the breakfast table. Only this time, the knock was on the back door. It was the landlord, Mr. Padgett, and he could see us sitting at the table.

Mr. Padgett looked almost as sad as Mother and Aunt

Catherine did when he broke the news. "I'm sorry, Mrs. Manning. I can't carry you and your husband any more. Please, tell Arthur I wish things were different; but if you can't pay the $25 a month, you'll need to pack your things and be out by the end of the week."

With that he hurried away and jammed himself back into his black sedan.

I ran out the door yelling, "Hey, my dad will fix this. Stop. Don't kick us out."

I looked eye to eye at him as he sat in his car and I clung to his window. "I'm sorry, Artie. You're only a kid. You can't understand things like money and how bad this Depression is on everyone. If I let you stay, I'd have to let half a dozen others stay in their homes, too. I can't afford that. I wish I could magically make this different, but I can't."

"I wish I could make you disappear."

"Sometimes I wish that, too, Artie. It's hard times, and I wish I could disappear until it was all over or wake up and discover this was all a bad dream."

"I'm sorry, Mr. Padgett. I don't want to make you disappear."

"I know, Artie. It's okay. Hey, your mom tells me your working on some magic of your own. Keep at it, Artie, work hard. Things will turn out fine in the end. You never know, you could even end up right back here."

"I hope so," I said.

"Me, too, son. Me, too."

I didn't like solving mysteries. The first one I solved got me a spanking, and the second one got my family kicked out of our house. But, for the first time, our parents talked to us like we were men. They sat us down and Father said, "Living with two families under the same roof has been hard, but I think you've had fun, too. We hope you haven't minded this too much because both families are out on the street now."

"What does that mean? Are we going to live on the street? We could get run over out there. You told me I can't ever go in the street," said Sister.

"Don't anybody get upset. We won't be in the street. We are going to have to move, though. All of us are going to live with your grandparents," Mother said.

"What if they get kicked out of their house, too?" asked Leroy.

Uncle Lyle answered, "Don't worry about that. They own their house so no landlord will come knocking on the door for rent."

"We can answer the door anytime we want?"

"Yes, anytime you want," Aunt Catherine said.

Our grandparents lived downtown. While it wasn't close enough to walk there or visit every day, it wasn't too far from where we had been living. It was in the city, though, so everything there was different. There were more cars and more people. The houses weren't like ours. Our grandparents' house was part of a row house.

Row houses are rows of houses pushed up against each other. They share walls with a different family on each side. There wasn't a front yard, only steps leading right from the sidewalk to the front door. If it weren't for Grandmother's chair by the front door we would have had a hard time telling their house from all the rest. The house was okay, but there was almost no yard to play in. We loved our yard with its hill and apple tree and shed. This was going to be tough for us boys, for sure.

CHAPTER 11

Moving Day

Moving day turned out to be the next day. Our parents all knew it was coming and had thought through the details. Grandfather had a truck that he used to hawk vegetables and that was our moving van. The moms packed up the kitchen, and each of us kids was ordered to pack a knapsack with all of our things in it.

"I'm worried. How am I going to get Maggie on the truck?"

"Show up downstairs with your pack and Maggie. I'm sure Dad will let her on the truck," Tommy tried to assure me.

"Is this the same father that we have lived with all our lives? The one who thinks being a magician is stupid enough even without me trying to take Maggie with me just so I can saw her in half?"

"You could saw her in half and put half of her in your pack and half in mine," offered Leroy.

"Yeah, then you can figure out how to put her back together

later," Tommy said.

"Sneak her onto the truck. I'll help you," said Bucky.

When Grandfather arrived to pick up a load, I worked hard and kept a good attitude. Grandfather couldn't abide with complainers. One small grumble and he would say something like, "If you think that's bad, you should try sleeping in a foxhole or drinking water out of a muddy boot."

About the third load in, it was time for us kids to load our knapsacks and toys. Grandfather was drinking a glass of water and that gave us the chance to get Maggie on board. We laid her down in the bed of the truck, and we placed all of our sacks on top of her. Grandfather never even noticed. I knew that as long as she was with me, I would be a real magician someday.

It took most of the day to get our stuff moved. As we were piling the last of our things on the truck, Paul and her dad came over.

"Well, I guess we're out of here," Tommy said.

"We're sorry to see you go, boys. We'll miss you and your family around here," said Mr. Cox.

"Thank you, sir. We'll miss you all, too," I replied.

"This stinks worse than pigs and chickens. We never even got to saw Maggie in half!" Paul said.

"I know; it stinks big time. But we will figure out how to saw Maggie in half, just you wait," I said.

"Yeah, and maybe we'll even figure out how to put her back together again," Tommy said.

I left Tommy and Paul talking by the truck and started back toward the house. Mr. Cox called me over to him. "Artie, would you mind following me over to my house for a minute? I have something I want to show you before you pull out."

"Sure, Mr. Cox."

We sat down on his front porch and he handed me a box. "I have a little something for you, Artie. From what Pauline tells me, this could come in handy."

I could not believe what was in that box – a magic kit. It included a card trick, a magic cup, disappearing balls, a coin trick, a paddle trick and a finger chopper!

"Do you think your grandfather will have room on the truck for this?"

"Oh, I'm sure he will. Thank you so much, Mr. Cox. I can't believe you gave me this!"

"Well, it's just a little something. A man has to have a dream. Now, head on home before you get me in trouble."

I walked back to the truck, looking at my kit. It was amazing. Tommy and Paul were still standing there talking. They talked a long time – long enough that I made fun of him for talking to a girl until he told me to shut up and punched me in the shoulder.

As we climbed up on the truck, I felt a big lump in my throat. It was all I could do not to cry. For once I was thankful for Sister's incessant talking. You can't break down into tears when Sister is driving you crazy. I felt bad for her, though. She had no idea how different things were about to be for us.

"Are you kids ready to have some big, new adventures in the city? You're going to love it there – lots to do and see. And you know your grandparents are crazy about you. You'll probably be spoiled rotten by next week," Mother said.

We weren't convinced, but we tried not to let Mother know how sad we were. Every time we mentioned our house, she started to cry; and we never knew what to do with that. As we pulled away we waved goodbye to Paul. It was the saddest day ever.

CHAPTER 12

The New Adventure

Our grandparents were old. Mother told us they were in their sixties. She sat us down and gave us a speech. "Now, children, you have to be extra respectful to them. I want plenty of yes-sirs and yes-ma'ams. Remember, this is their home and you are not to go running through like a bunch of wild Indians. Use your inside voices."

Sister asked, "What if we are outside? Do we have to use our inside voices then?"

"No, of course not, Louise."

Tommy and I rolled our eyes at each other. Sister was ridiculous; but Mom made it sound like loud noises could kill our grandparents or something, so for a couple of days I was careful.

I discovered that, for old people, they were pretty sturdy. Grandfather sold vegetables from his truck every other day and Grandmother took in sewing. They were hard working people and to me, it looked like they were rich. We didn't know many people who owned their own houses, except for Paul's family across the street from us and, of course, the doctor.

Grandmother said they weren't rich, but were doing okay.

Okay was great by us. We settled in quickly and liked it. We could answer the door and there was enough food to eat.

We older boys bunked in together and Edgar and Louise had little pallets for their beds in the corners of their parents' rooms. I threw my knapsack on the floor of our room and started chopping fingers. It was pretty chintzy, but it worked. It looked like a miniature guillotine. I would ask someone from the audience (or in this case my bedroom) to put their finger in the top opening. Then I would roll up some paper or a soft stick and put it through the bottom hole. I'd push the top down and chop the paper clean through, leaving the finger uninjured.

The rest of the tricks were going to take a little more practice than this one, but they would have to wait because Grandfather called us all downstairs.

"Children, I have a little something for you. You live in the city now. Things are different here. There is a lot of pavement and not much grass. Kids around here get around on roller skates and you should, too. The children of one of my customers have all grown up and have no need for skates, so he traded them to me for fruit and vegetables. Let's go outside and strap them on and see how you do."

Soon we went everywhere on skates. I was a natural. In no time, I could skate backwards and on one foot, and I was fast like lightening.

Our ready-made street hockey team of Tommy and me and the cousins helped us to make friends with other boys in the neighborhood. Everyone traveled on roller skates with a skate key on a string around their neck.

Grandfather was right – it was different here. We played on the streets all the time instead of in the woods or on vacant lots like we used to. Grown-ups would sit around on the front steps and watch us after dinner. Not too bad a place, but not exactly home.

Uncle Lyle was a handy man and could fix or build anything. It didn't take long for him to find work in the city – even if it was odd jobs.

Father took longer. He continued to go out daily and look for work. He told us he "pounded the pavement" from sun up 'til sun down. He was open to doing anything. He had done all kinds of stuff in the past, but nothing specialized.

Two weeks passed and then one afternoon I heard Father whistling as he came into the house. As I peeked down the stairs I saw him pull Mother up off her chair and dance her around the room.

"Louise, today I walked clear across town looking for work. I waited in line after line for work details and wasn't picked for anything. I was tired and discouraged. I went to go get a cup of coffee, and when I sat down there was a familiar face at the end of the counter. It was Mr. Humphrey, Artie's and Tommy's favorite cab driver."

"Land sakes, Arthur. What are the chances of that?"

"Before I knew it, we were in deep discussion. Mr. Humphrey is expanding his cab company to five cabs and is looking for another driver. He hired me just like that."

With our fathers both working again, I wondered if someday we could return to our house in the old neighborhood. Maybe someday Bucky, Leroy, Edgar and William would have their own house, too. For now, having our cousins around was great (except for the wet bed part). With six boys, you could get a game up of just about anything and the chores got split up that many more ways.

The new cab was scheduled to be ready in two weeks. Money would soon be coming in again. The only bad part about Father's new job was that it officially put an end to our "Hail a

Cab" game. If we wanted to endanger our lives, all we needed to do was give a whistle and see Father's face as he stepped out of his cab. It might be the last thing we'd ever see.

CHAPTER 13

Doing Chores with Speed and Style

Grandmother handed each of us a chore list to do while she and the mothers went to the market. We beat rugs and washed windows. Sister even had work to do. She swept the stoop and helped fold the laundry. Grandmother wanted us to polish the woodwork in the house, especially get the fingerprints off the railing going down the stairs.

Leroy said to Edgar, "I think the best way to do this railing is slide down it."

"You're going to break something for sure," said William.

"Nah, watch this."

Leroy mounted the railing like he was getting on a horse. He wobbled a bit at first and then down he went. It wasn't graceful. He was wearing shorts so his legs kept sticking and making a horrible screeching sound.

"You're doing it wrong," Bucky said. He took his dust rag and rubbed polish up and down the railing and then got on himself. Whoosh, down he went like a blur. Leroy ran up and changed to pants and we all got in line to polish the railing. Sister came around the corner and saw us, she wanted to help.

We got the laundry basket and put it at the bottom of the railing and slid Sister into it. She loved it – we all did; but soon it wasn't enough.

"We need to take it up a notch. We can turn the stairs into a toboggan run," I said.

Tommy and I took the mattress off our bed and moved it to the top of the stairs. We slid down on it, like a sled, but it was too slow. Edgar and Leroy quickly polished the steps and we tried it again. We flew down, laughing and screaming all the way, until we crashed into the front door.

"I'm not sure how many times I can do that without cracking my head open," Tommy said.

"Uh, once. Look at that goose egg on your forehead!" I said.

"The door doesn't look much better," said William.

"That's it, Dad's going to murder us," Leroy shouted.

"We can fix this. Edgar, get a rag and we'll buff out that mark on the door. Tommy, put your ball cap on. Nobody will be the wiser," I said.

Tommy came downstairs wearing his cap and holding a bunch of pillows. "We'll put these in front of the door so nobody will get hurt again."

Soon we went down two at a time. On Bucky and William's turn, Tommy and I gave them an extra treat. As they slid down the stairs, we opened the front door and they landed right out on the stoop. Our timing was perfect. Grandmother and our moms were arriving home and barely escaped being plowed down by our mattress-sled.

We held our breath and stared at them, with the fresh knowledge that the bump on Tommy's head would need no further explanation.

Grandmother clutched her bag in both arms like her life

depended on it and then, suddenly, burst into laughter. "I do declare, I haven't seen this much life around here in ages. Guess it's time you brushed things off and put my house back in order."

Our moms looked at us with the kind of look that made us know we'd gotten off easy. I hugged Grandmother, and this time we did clean up.

CHAPTER 14

The Circus Comes to Town

After lunch, we went skating. A good thing about living in the city was there was nothing but concrete and streetcar lines here, and that made skating great. We weren't in the heart of the city, so there weren't too many cars to watch out for either.

Today we went farther from our grandparents' home than we ever had before. We found a ballpark, a couple of bars, a diner and even a hotel. We had seen rooming houses, but never a hotel. There were taxicabs dropping off and picking up people at the train station. This was a big station, not like the little stop down the street from our old house. We sat and watched the train come and go. This was the same train that could take us back to our old neighborhood in about twenty minutes, but it seemed like we were much farther away than that twenty-minute train ride.

"Boys," called a man in a jacket with B&O emblazoned on the shoulder. "I've never seen you fellows down here before. You new in town?"

"Yes sir, pretty new. We just moved in with our grandparents," said Tommy.

"Well, you picked a good time to do that. Today the circus comes to town. The train will be here in two hours, and then the circus will unload and parade to the fair grounds. Have you ever seen an elephant before?"

"Only in books. We've never seen a real, live one," said Bucky.

"You'll see elephants and a whole lot more if you stick around."

But we couldn't stick around. We were due back home and we couldn't risk waiting. We sped off on our skates as fast as we could toward home. Bursting in the house, we all started talking at once.

Our moms calmed us down long enough for me to spit out our dilemma between gasping for breath. "Mom, the circus, it's coming, train station, got to get back there."

"We'll all go," said Mother. "Let's get Louise and head on down."

It took forever for Aunt Catherine and Mother to gather Sister up and be ready to go. We thought for sure that the elephants would be long gone before we ever got there. The mothers had consented to let us skate if we would stay together, but we had to keep skating in circles to go slow enough for them and Sister.

As we neared the station we heard the train's whistle. We looked at our mothers with the saddest, most pitiful looks we could muster, and they sent us off ahead. We tore down the street, weaving in and out of people and dogs and arrived at the train station in time to see the train puffing its way up the track towards us. There were kids everywhere. Everyone wanted to get a look at the circus.

It was a long train and it took a while to pull in and stop.

The engineer waved and we could see people in the front cars. The back cars were more like boxes. We were sure that the elephants and big cats would be in some of those.

"We have to get closer," I said. And with that, I wiggled through the crowd with Tommy and the guys close behind me. It took forever for the doors to open – well, maybe two or three minutes. Finally, out came a man wearing the oddest suit I had ever seen. He looked like a penguin with a long tail down the back of his coat. It was strange, but wonderful.

He raised a megaphone to his mouth. "Ladies and gentlemen, boys and girls, thank you for this kind reception that you have provided for us today. We look forward to amazing you with sights and wonders from all over the globe. We look forward to presenting to you the greatest show your eyes have ever beheld."

Then he bowed so low he could have tied his shoes, all the while pointing with his arm to the rear of the train. With a loud thud a boxcar door dropped open.

"Wow," I squealed, "that's the biggest elephant I have ever seen!"

"It's the only elephant you have ever seen," Tommy saw fit to remind me.

But, no matter, it was all so exciting that I didn't even take the time to punch Tommy in the arm. The elephant lumbered down the plank being led by a man holding nothing but a stick. The elephant wrapped his trunk around the stick and followed him.

"I can't even get a dog to follow me on a leash," Leroy said.

Before long there were horses with ladies riding on them and wheeled cages with tigers in them parading down the street following the elephant toward the edge of town where they were to set up their circus tents. We saw a clown riding the tiniest bicycle ever and a man on stilts that must have been eight feet tall. This was probably the closest we would get to going to the circus. That would have to be okay with us; besides, we were sure it couldn't be better than this.

It took a long time to empty that train, but we waited. We didn't want to miss anything. Finally, two men in overalls got out and nailed posters to the wall telling all about the circus. Then they nailed up a small paper that said "Help Wanted." They needed help cleaning animal stalls and picking up trash. We read each word with excitement – maybe we could work at the circus. It was the first time that I can remember reading coming in handy. I ripped the paper off the wall, stuffed it in my pocket and went home with the family.

William and I decided it was best to ask the fathers about our job possibilities. Mothers have such a way of seeing the bad side of things. They're afraid we're going to get hurt or die or something. So, we waited.

At dinner, all anybody talked about was the circus parade. Sister loved the horses and wanted one that she could ride.

Grandfather laughed, "You're a might on the small side to ride one of those. When I was young, I went to a circus. Lots of excitement, animals, games, prizes to be won. But, there were a lot of shady characters – flimflam men looking for an easy mark."

Tommy and I looked at each other and then over at Bucky and William.

"We'll be fine," Leroy stated. "None of us is named Mark."

Tommy and I shook our heads. This wasn't going to help our cause. We needed a plan.

The next morning, we did our chores without complaining and hoped that we could go out to play quickly. Mother said we could, but warned us not to go down to the train station. She didn't think it was suitable for children to hang around there.

"Yes, ma'am," we replied with our best manners. "We won't go to the train station."

"Have fun," she said as we strapped on our skates. "And, be back by 1:00 for lunch."

"That was a close one," I said.

"What do you mean?" asked William.

"They said we couldn't go to the train station but didn't say anything about the circus grounds. We didn't have to lie."

Our plan was to go right to the circus grounds and see for ourselves how safe we knew it would be and how trustworthy all the people who worked there surely were.

The circus grounds were swarming with activity. Our hearts were beating as fast from excitement as they were from skating. There were animal pens being constructed and tents going up. I have never seen so many trailers and cages. It was like a little city was being built right before our eyes.

Leroy said, "I think Grandfather was right. A lot of the men do look scary." Then he added, "I hope we can work here."

"You're weird, Leroy. These guys are sweaty and dirty. That's all," said Tommy.

CHAPTER 15

The Interview

The help-wanted sign said to apply in person at the manager's trailer. There were a lot of trailers lined up and none had a sign on it. We started knocking on doors and hoped for the best.

There was a feeling of danger behind every door – something we were not accustomed to at all. The sharp sound of a hammer hitting a stake made us jump out of our skin. "I think Grandfather has gotten into our heads," William said.

The first trailer had the door propped open enough for us to see inside the dimly lit room. We stuck our heads in and were greeted by a smell that was something like a mix of cooked cabbage and dirty socks. "This is my kind of place," Leroy said.

The second one we came to had a smell that reminded me of the time we had a dead rat stuck under our house. Not even Leroy was willing to knock.

At the next trailer when we heard someone coming toward the door, we weren't sure if we were disappointed or relieved.

This was a much scarier place than we had figured.

A young woman with a huge snake draped around her shoulders opened the door and asked if she could help us. We couldn't find our tongues. We stood there like idiots with our mouths open and our eyes fixed on the snake.

She burst out laughing. "What's the matter, boys? Cat got your tongue?" she asked while she lifted the snake's head in our direction.

Tommy managed to utter a few words. "We're looking for, we're looking for, we're looking for, the ma…ma…manager."

She took her snake's head in her left hand and pointed with it. "Next trailer," she said and closed the door.

We stood there staring at her door, unable to move.

"She was nice," Leroy said.

We all laughed and moved on to the next trailer. The door opened and the man who had worn the fancy suit stood in front of us.

"Gentlemen, won't you come in. What can I do for you this fine day?"

All of us filed into his trailer, knowing that our moms would have had a fit, if only they had known.

"Well, sir," I offered, "we saw the flyer down at the station and we want to apply for jobs."

"You boys look pretty young, and you look like city boys. City boys may not be able to cut it here."

"Oh, we're not city boys. We're living in the city with our grandparents for a while. We're more country boys – town boys. We can work real hard," Tommy said.

"Well, I make it a practice never to hire on hands that are less than 12 years old."

"William and I are 13, and Tommy and Bucky here are 12," I lied. It wasn't a big lie. I was getting ready to turn 12 in a couple months, and William was 13. Plus, I couldn't get the job without Tommy and Bucky. Bucky was big for his age and he looked older than I do, but he was 11 and Tommy was only 10. This meant, of course, that Edgar and Leroy couldn't get jobs, as they were 7 and 9. There was no way I could lie for all of us, it was too risky.

Leroy was shooting arrows out of his eyes at me, but he didn't say a word. Edgar, as usual, didn't know what was going on but stayed surprisingly quiet as he looked around the room.

"I might be able to put four of you to work. By the way, I'm Mr. Santamaria, the circus master."

"It's nice to meet you," we all said talking over each other. Well, not all of us – Edgar was busy trying to tie his shoelace; and Leroy looked like he wanted to cry and punch somebody at the same time.

"If you don't mind," Tommy interrupted. "I have a question for you. Our grandparents and especially our mothers are going to want to know – do you have any flimflam men working here?"

Mr. Santamaria asked, "That's a strange question. Are you looking for a flimflam man?"

William added, "Grandfather warned us that confidence men often are part of the circus, so we thought if we could tell them we made sure there are none here that would go a long way with our folks."

"No need to worry about that here," he said with a laugh that made me a touch nervous. "You four older boys can report here tomorrow morning bright and early – 7:00 AM. You've got yourselves a job. Sorry for you two little guys, maybe next time."

Leroy looked sad while Edgar didn't seem to realize what had happened. Leroy told him, "Edgar, we can't work at the circus. Don't you get it? We're too little."

"That's okay, Leroy. We can stay home and play. Who wants to work anyway?"

We had to find a way to make them feel better, especially Leroy, so we wandered around the grounds. It might be their last chance to see circus people and we wanted to help them have a little excitement.

We came across a pen with a lot of little dogs in it. There was a man working with them and making them jump through hoops and climb up ladders. He seemed like a kind man – nothing flim-flammy about him. He smiled at us while we watched him. We let Leroy and Edgar get the closest so that they would feel special. After a while the man asked if we like dogs.

"We love them, especially Leroy and Edgar," William said.

And with that the man invited those two to come in and try their hand at doing tricks with the dogs. Leroy had them jumping through hoops over and over again. Edgar made them run behind him and jump over little fences and push a baby carriage. It was the right thing to ease the pain of not being real circus workers like the rest of us.

Our stomachs started growling, so we went home for lunch. We had to tell our folks about our new jobs. This time the plan was simple – we would tell them everything. We were sure William and Tommy's investigation into the presence of flimflam men working at the circus would smooth the way for us to work there.

After dinner was over, Father said we boys could be excused. We asked if we could talk and told them all about our adventure to the circus. We told them of the helpful snake lady and the kind dog trainer and the people that were working hard. We told them about Mr. Santamaria, but we didn't tell them that we lied about our age.

Grandmother looked nervous as she raised her napkin to her face – in fact, all the grown-ups looked nervous.

Tommy spoke up, "We asked them if there were flimflam men there. We knew you'd worry about that. Good news – there aren't any. Mr. Santamaria said so."

"Oh, you asked about that, did you?" said Grandfather. His tone made it hard to tell if he was pleased that we had investigated the possibility or if he was making fun of us.

"Let's make things clear and certain. It sounds to me like you already accepted the jobs. Is that right?" asked Aunt Catherine.

"Yes, that's right. Well, sort of right. We're supposed to start work tomorrow morning," said William.

"He means the four of them got jobs. Edgar and I are too little," added Leroy.

We all sat quietly for a while and then Father and Uncle Lyle excused us from the table to wait upstairs while the parents talked. I hated those times – it seemed like our very lives were hanging in the balance. I was sure that I would never leave my children hanging when I was a father. And, I would never let my children miss out on working at a fine job like the circus.

After a very long hour we were called back downstairs. We filed into the room like crooks going into a line-up. We sat down and waited for them to speak.

"Well, well," Uncle Lyle said. "You boys have had quite a day. I'm glad you made it there and back safely, but you need to learn to tell your mothers exactly where you are going. Suppose something had happened or we needed you right away. You have to act more responsibly, including not taking Edgar so far from home."

"You need to learn to think things through," said Father.

"Yes sir. We will," we all said.

I had a bad feeling. We don't get these kinds of talks before we get a yes from our parents. These are the talks you get to explain a no.

Then Father began, "Tomorrow morning after breakfast I will accompany you four boys to see Mr. Santamaria. I'll explain to him how you sneaked over to the circus without permission and applied for a job without your parents knowing anything about it. Then you will tell him that you are sorry for taking up his time without having been responsible enough to make sure it was cleared by your parents. If at that point, he forgives you and is willing to take a chance on you four hooligans, then it's okay with us if you work for him this summer."

Our eyes had lowered to the floor as we were being chewed out. Our dreams were being suffocated slowly by Uncle Lyle's and Father's words. Then, without warning, we could breathe again. We all jumped up and thanked our parents. We assured them that we wouldn't let them down, that we'd be honest with them and respect them. We'd act like men. Then it hit me.

I softly spoke up, "Dad, I'm not sure we can take the jobs. There's one more thing that we didn't tell you, and if we're going to be responsible men, then you need to know...... I lied about how old Tommy, Bucky and I are. Mr. Santamaria said he needed us to be 12, so I said I was 13 and that Tommy and Bucky were 12. It just kind of came out of my mouth. I wanted the job so bad."

"Bad enough to lie? You have to understand how important it is to always tell the truth," Dad said.

"If it's so important to be honest, how come it's so easy to lie?"

"It seems easy to try to make things work for you by not telling the truth. Somehow you think that you can make people overlook the obstacle by lying, but it comes back to you. One lie leads to another and before you know it, you're in deep trouble. How would Mr. Santamaria feel if after you'd been working for him a while he found out that you lied to him? He'd think that you didn't respect him enough to argue your case with the truth or accept his standard. That's not a very good way to start out, is it?"

I looked at my mom and she said, "I guess you know what you need to do, don't you?"

And I did. Not only had I lied, but I had made all the guys a part of it. I had to make it right and hope for the best. How do I manage to mess things up so badly?

Morning came and we all ate breakfast before our first day of work – at least we hoped we would be working. Father didn't ask about my plan for talking to Mr. Santamaria. I had hoped that he would, but it seemed he was letting me handle this one. I didn't want to handle this one. The more I tried to handle, the more I realized that I needed my father.

Confessing things to an adult is not fun. Mr. Santamaria agreed with all our fathers' comments. He told us that his time is valuable and that we should be respectful of that and that he couldn't abide being lied to. But, he also said he liked it when men owned up to their faults and set things straight, so we could have the job – all four of us – at least on a trial basis to see if we could handle it. "People who are contrite deserve another chance," he said.

And with that, he and Father shook hands and our first workday began. I wanted to give Father a hug and tell him how glad I was that he was letting us work here. I wanted to thank him and tell him I wouldn't let him down and I'd make him proud of me, but it seemed like a handshake was the best way to let him know how I felt. I walked up to him and gave him the firmest handshake I could; and even though he said nothing, his look told me that he was indeed proud of me.

CHAPTER 16

Working Men

Three other boys were starting work that day. They were a little older than us, but of course no one had circus experience, so we all started out at the bottom. And I do mean the bottom. There are a lot of animals in the circus and that means there is a lot of poop. There are cages with poop in them. There are stables with poop in them. The circus tents have poop in them. And there is poop on the bottom of people's shoes.

Our main job was to get the poop picked up and put it in the poop place so that the workers and guests didn't have to step in it. We were all assigned different areas to do poop patrol. The three boys were split up and were assigned the dog pen, the common areas and the circus tent. They would patrol for trash and poop, feed and walk the dogs, and rake the common areas and tent area. They also did odd jobs for Mr. Santamaria and brought lunch to the regular circus workers. William and Bucky were big guys; their jobs were to bring the feedbags into the horse, elephant and tiger areas. They would deliver the bags and portion out the food for the trainers. They were also used as gophers – they would be sent to "go for" this and "go for" that.

Tommy and I were the last two to be assigned. Mr. Santamaria said that he had a special job for the one who was concerned about the flimflam men and the one that had to 'fess up to lying. "You two will have the privilege of working with the tigers, horses and the elephants. How do you feel about that?"

We could barely believe our ears. "Thank you, thank you, Mr. Santamaria. We feel great about that. Who wouldn't want to work with those big animals! When can we meet them?"

"Well, you won't be working directly with the animals. These animals are dangerous and it takes years to be able to work with a tiger or an elephant. You will be working in their areas while they are trained and exercised."

With that, Mr. Santamaria handed the other boys pails and rakes and shovels. He told Bucky and William where to find the food supplies and introduced them to the stable manager. Then he turned to us and directed us to the biggest bucket and shovel I have ever seen. We would be picking up the biggest poop of all.

"There you go. This ought to take care of the waste. Make sure you pick up all of it. You don't want to smell this stuff after it's been baking in the sun for a while."

He handed us our schedules and off we went to meet our supervisors. Tommy and I kept looking at each other as we walked toward the horse stalls. What started out as a dream job might not be all we thought it would be.

The horse stalls smelled like hay and poop. It was a weird blend of sweet and stinky, but at least we would be around horses. They were pretty friendly as was the stable-keeper. He told us what to do and we began.

"This isn't too bad," we kept telling each other.

Next on our schedule were the tiger cages. We wanted to peek into the tent and watch the trainer working with the big cats, but we had to clean the cages. This was worse than the horses. We scooped and hosed down everything and were directed to Poop Hill where we deposited the waste. We could hear the cats and the trainers. It was a little like torture not to be able to stop and look in, but we were forced to be responsible. We had to make a good showing of it for our father and Mr. Santamaria.

The sun was beating down hard on us, and sweat was breaking out across our foreheads as we headed to the elephant area. There was a total of three elephants in this circus, and nothing could have prepared us for how much they poop. The wind had picked up a little, so as we approached, we had a feeling that there would be plenty for us to do.

Two elephants were tethered in their pen, and the trainer was hosing down the other one. It seems elephants like to roll in the dirt; and that means whatever is in the dirt, for instance their own poop, gets on them. They can get pretty stinky. That is why, we were told, our job is so important. Nobody wants to come to the circus and smell dirty elephants. While one elephant was being washed and the other two were tethered, we were directed to start scooping.

Everywhere we looked there were brown piles that had been baking in the sun all morning. "Hum, sunbaked brownies," I said.

Tommy looked at me and shook his head. Then he looked down at our huge bucket as we filled it with the foulest smell ever and said, "I wonder what elephants eat to make this much stinky poop. We'll have to ask Bucky or William."

"I don't think it's all about the what. It has to be partly about the how much. Think about it. When we eat all day long, how much do we go? It's so much food to make so little..."

Tommy cut me off mid-sentence, "You're disgusting, Artie."

"Maybe we should try measuring the in and out sometime, or at least the out. Sounds like a good science project."

"You can leave me out of that project. I think the heat is getting to you," said Tommy.

We filled our bucket and dragged it away, only to return to fill it two more times. That was our day. Show up by 7:00. Work with poop until 10:30 or 11:00 and then head home. The circus would be in town for 10 days; we would be working for 11. The extra day was to help clean up as they broke down the circus.

At the end of our first day, we met with Mr. Santamaria. He asked us how we liked being working men, and of course we said we liked it fine. He smiled and said he'd see us tomorrow.

Bucky and William were waiting for us, so the four of us could walk home together. They smelled sweaty, but we smelled worse. William kept going on and on about how great their job was. He actually got to touch an elephant and the trainer told him that he'd show him the ropes of working at the circus. Everybody liked William. He was easy-going and helpful and always had a smile on his face. It didn't hurt any that he was strong for his age. He looked like a 15-year-old instead of the 13-year-old that he was.

Bucky was quick to add, "I got to touch an elephant, too. This is the best job in the world. How did you guys like your jobs?"

"Well," Tommy began, "there was plenty to do. The horse guy is nice and we got to pet the horses."

"It smells like you were plenty busy. How about you guys stay down-wind of us. My eyes are starting to burn," Bucky said.

And that's the way it was. Bucky and William had the glamour jobs. Tommy and I got poop.

Our stomachs were growling as loud as the tigers by the time we walked into the kitchen. The smell of Mother's homemade bread made us forget about our jobs, and we slipped into our chairs at the table. Grandmother greeted us from the sink where she stood snapping beans. Drying off her hands, she said, "Now you boys don't forget your manners. Give Grandmother a hug before you head over to wash up for lunch."

William and Bucky hugged her and she said with a smile, "My, my, don't you two have the smell of working men."

Then Tommy and I reached out for a hug and Grandmother nearly fainted. "I don't have to ask what you did today. Head on into the washroom, take those clothes off, and wash yourselves from head to toe. We may need to bury those overalls."

You know you smell bad when your grandmother won't hug you. That's the ultimate test. But after a good scrubbing, she was happy to give us a hug, let us sit at the table with the family, and eat some of Mother's bread with jelly.

Lunch helped us forget all the stinky parts of our jobs. As Grandmother, Aunt Catherine and Mother sat down with us and wanted to hear all about our day, nothing but fun and excitement came to our minds. Our day. That's what our mothers ask our fathers. How was your day dear? We were men!

Aunt Catherine told Bucky and William, "By the time the circus pulls out of town, you two are going to have big muscles from hauling all the feed."

Then Mother looked at Tommy and me. I could see her searching for the right words. "You two boys will be getting stronger and stronger, too," she said.

"Yeah," Bucky said. "They were plenty strong today! William and I could barely stand walking with them!"

Even Tommy and I laughed. I guess we had to since everyone

else did.

"Now, Bucky," Aunt Catherine added. "Any job that's an honest job is a good job, and I'm sure the boys are happy to be working at the circus."

And, we were. Our heads were full of dreams of payday and circus animals. Mr. Santamaria had not mentioned if we would be able to actually see the circus, but I thought if we worked hard, maybe we would. Dreams of being a magician kept coming into my mind, too. There must be a magician in the circus somewhere among all those performers. If he was there, I would find him.

In celebration of our first day of work, we were released from our daily chores. My first thought went to Maggie. I hadn't paid any attention to her lately. She had been waiting patiently in the corner of our bedroom for me to find time for her. The only magic she had been involved in was her ability to frighten Edgar and Sister. When the sun was almost down and our room filled with the shadows accentuated by the window curtains blowing in the breeze, they were convinced that they had seen her move. They wouldn't even go in our room by themselves.

This could have created a big problem for me with keeping Maggie, but Bucky knew how to handle his little brother, so he never complained. He was always on my side. William was loyal, too, but sometimes he would place other things above his loyalty – things like honesty and concern for his little brothers. I liked being around him, but Bucky was my buddy. Bucky and Tommy, that is.

CHAPTER 17

Job Benefits

Mother fixed us pancakes with King Syrup to give us, as she said, "an appropriate start to the day." The familiar lion on the label was the closest breakfast food she could come up with that had anything to do with a circus. I wasn't quite sure why that seemed important to her, but she happily hummed while she served us.

Since yesterday, a lot of posters advertising the circus had sprung up around town. We were proud to be part of it all and secretly relieved that we got in on this job early before more qualified people applied. We decided to call ourselves circus folk, as that sounded way more prestigious than did our 11-day contract. Besides, we liked the sound of it.

We arrived on the grounds the same time the other three guys did. They were only a couple of years older than us, but they acted like they were God's gift to the circus. One of them said, "I guess anybody can work here, even little boys who need their mommies to wipe their noses."

"Hey, do you think you can get your work done before it's nap time?" another jeered.

"Who do you think you're talking to?" asked Bucky. "William could clean your clock with one hand tied behind his back."

William stepped up. "I don't think that'll be necessary, Bucky. These guys are ribbing us. Aren't you?"

The snake lady stepped out of her trailer and our confrontation was over. My heart was beating out of my chest. I didn't want to fight anybody, especially not somebody that was so much bigger than me. It would be a shame to have my neck broken so early in my new job.

When we met the snake lady, Leroy commented that she seemed nice; and it turned out that she was. She invited us to stop by her trailer at the end of our shift for something cold to drink. That sounded good to us, as we remembered how hot and thirsty we were after our first day of work.

Bucky and William headed to the feed storage, and Tommy and I went to get our huge bucket and shovel. We looked forward to our first job – the horses. We didn't mind the smell in the stable – at least as compared to the elephants and tigers. In the stable, there was a mix of sweet smelling hay with the poop and it hadn't been baking in the sun.

Smithy, the stable manager, was brushing down one of the horses. He looked up and nodded and started talking like we had been in a conversation with him already.

"You take the good with the bad," he said without looking up. "The horses are good, strong animals. They're well suited for man to use for work and transportation. They're loyal. These are the good qualities that make dealing with their dung bearable."

Of course, that was easy for him to say, since we were the ones who dealt with it.

Tommy and I took every opportunity to make friends with this soft-spoken man. We liked hearing him talk about the horses. He had a nice way about him – the kind of manner that makes you feel like you have always known him. He told us that his name wasn't Smithy. People just called him that since his blacksmith skills were helpful with caring for the horses.

The tiger cage cleanup went fast. The tigers were out of their cages like yesterday so we could scoop and hose things down easily.

Then, on to the elephants; this is where we really earned our money. Again, we were amazed at how much elephant poop was there and how big it was.

"Remember Mrs. Taylor's pies that she would bake and put on her back porch to cool?" Tommy asked.

"Yeah, they didn't smell anything like this though."

"We used to hang around her yard hoping she'd give us a piece. Looking around here, each pile of poop looks like a burnt pie."

"There must be dozens of them, but I don't want a piece," I said.

Gerome the elephant handler walked up. "No, you don't want a piece of that. But if you didn't understand before why dung is sometimes called a pie, I guess you do now. Each elephant can give you 100 pounds of dung a day, so you'll never lack for work around here."

It took us more time to clean up the elephant area than the tiger and horse areas combined. And the smell, the smell was horrible. Even though there was hay all around like in the horse stalls, it wasn't enough to counteract the amount of elephant waste, especially on a hot July day with the sun beating down.

As I saw Gerome pull out a sandwich and start eating it, I asked Tommy, "Do you think we could get used to this enough to be able to eat our lunch out here?"

"Probably not in 11 days."

"I'll tell you what. If you can eat your whole lunch out here without puking, I'll do all of your chores at home for a week."

That was probably the safest bet I ever made, as I could maneuver Tommy out of his dessert just by talking about things that smell bad.

At long last we were heading to the snake lady's trailer for our much-needed cold drink. She greeted us warmly and we filed into her trailer. It was nice inside. It didn't look like the trailer of someone who would wear a snake around her shoulders. There were lace doilies on the back of the furniture and pictures of normal-looking people on the dresser. There was a little hot plate with a pot of water on it and a pitcher of lemonade that she made for us boys. There was even a jar of candy. The only thing that concerned me was there was not a snake in sight.

Not seeing the snake made me nervous. Where was he? Was he in a cage somewhere? Did he slither around the trailer and do whatever it is that snakes like to do? Would I sit down for a drink of lemonade only to find out that the snake likes lemonade, too, and would just as soon squeeze the life out of me to get mine? Was this a trap? Tommy looked nervous, too; but Bucky and William, who had arrived before us, looked quite at ease. They were already sipping on their drinks when we showed up.

"Glad you boys could stop in. Have a seat across from your cousins, if they are your cousins," she said with a grin.

"Thanks, and they are our cousins. We didn't lie about that," I said.

"By the way, my name is Matilda Santamaria; but you can call me Miss Tillie. How do you like working here so far?" she asked as she poured our drinks.

We told her we loved the work. We talked and talked, and soon we noticed something that we hadn't noticed before. Miss Tillie was kind of young. Our first impression of her had been a blur of a person holding a huge snake, but now we could see that she was young and pretty. She wasn't nearly as old as our mothers, but she was older than us for sure. That must have put her somewhere around twenty.

We learned that she had little brothers about our age and she missed them a lot. She showed us an old picture of them with her and two people who must have been her parents. The smile on her face faded as she stared at the picture, her fingers gliding over it with a strange gentleness. William cleared his throat and asked about her brothers.

"Oh," she said, "they died of the fever a few years back. Momma got the fever and then the boys. I'm glad Momma passed first. It would have broken her heart to see her boys pass on. That left my father and me. After a while, Father decided that he and I couldn't stay in the house any more. I think his heart was broken. Everywhere around the house were reminders of my mother. It was more than he could take."

With every word, she looked younger and younger. There was something about the way she told us the story that made her seem like she could be somebody we went to school with or who lived down the street. We all sat quietly, not knowing what to say as Miss Tillie told her story. Then all of a sudden, Tommy jumped so high he knocked his chair over. It was a good thing we had finished our drinks, because he knocked the table, too, and in the process revealed that huge snake crawling right under where we had been sitting. This was too much for Bucky, William and Miss Tillie, who had hoped for such an occurrence. Soon the trailer was filled with laughter, and we knew that we had made a friend.

CHAPTER 18

Running Away with the Circus

Every day was the same at the circus – arrive early, do our chores, and have lemonade with Tillie. By the third day we had dropped the "Miss" and she became Tillie. She and her father had been with the circus since she was 12.

I don't know why, but it surprised us to find out that Mr. Santamaria was Tillie's dad. I guess you don't think about a girl hanging around with a snake as having parents.

It was easy to see that Mr. Santamaria's golden voice and strong work ethic had made him a shoe-in for the job of Ring Master. He was also an organizational genius and ran the circus like a business.

Tillie was helping us get used to her snake. He wasn't poisonous, she assured us; but he does like to hug, she would add with a smile. By the end of a week we were all being hugged by Linus. Linus was a ball python and almost four feet long. It was pretty nifty having a snake around you. His skin was smooth and cool-to-the-touch but warmed up as he slithered

101

over us.

"I thought that snakes would be slimy," Tillie told us. "When my dad told me we were going to be traveling with the circus, and that I would be handling snakes, I immediately started crying. I knew that snakes were the most disgusting creatures on earth – so sneaky and slithery. I hated them. But Dad was patient with me and before I knew it, I was happy to have them as pets. Linus was my first snake. He's grown about to full size now. He has the best disposition and I'm sure he likes to play jokes on people as much as I do. He's the perfect pet."

"Why would anyone want their 12-year old daughter to handle snakes?" Bucky asked.

"It's not like he was looking for a snake-handler job for me. It just worked out that way. Circus people are a tight group. This circus was visiting our town a few months after the boys died; and Dad thought it would cheer me up to see a circus, so we went. The next day there was a fire in one of the trailers and the ringmaster died. Dad said he was compelled to come and help the performers, because when I watched them I had finally smiled again and even laughed out loud. He took them some fruit and helped rake out the debris from the fire. They didn't understand why he would come and help; but when he told them about the joy that he had seen on my face the night before, there was an instant connection. To make a long story short, my dad and I ran away with the circus; and we are all one family now."

"How long have you been with them?" William asked.

"It's been five years. We love it here. Dad says that he may have come to help them, but it was they who rescued us. What about you guys? What's your story?"

I had never thought of us as having a story before, but I guess everyone has one. Ours was just short. We told Tillie about how we had to move in with our grandparents and how we missed the old neighborhood. We told how we smuggled Maggie onto Grandfather's truck on moving day. When we explained "Hail a Cab" and that our father now drove a cab for a living, I thought she would blow lemonade out of her nose from laughing at us.

"It sounds like you have more of a story than you think," she remarked.

"Well, it's mostly a story about getting in trouble. We do that real good," Tommy said.

"You mean you do that well," Tillie corrected.

"Yeah, isn't that what I said?"

CHAPTER 19

The Big Show

Every passing day, we became more and more obsessed with the possibility of actually seeing the circus. The weekend was coming and there would be three big performances. Mr. Santamaria had not mentioned anything about us seeing one. All he said was be sure you're on time Saturday morning. There's going to be a lot of trash to pick up after Friday night's show.

"I guess that means we won't be seeing the show on Friday," I muttered.

"There are still two on Saturday," William said with a hopeful smile.

Poor William didn't get it. "Why would they let us boys in for free while there are paying customers out there? It doesn't matter anyway. We've practically seen it all during rehearsals. What's the difference," I said, almost even convincing myself.

"Boys," bellowed Mr. Santamaria as he and Tillie walked

toward us.

"Well, lads, it's almost over. We pull out on Sunday. Now, with an evening show and a matinee tomorrow, in addition to your normal reporting time, I'm going to need you for an extra duty to make things spick and span. Meet back here again at 1:30. Then, we'll see you on Sunday morning for clean up before we pull out."

"But, sir," William said. "The matinee starts at 2:00. We won't have anything to clean up yet. Shouldn't we come back later, maybe in between shows?"

"Hum, I think you're right about that. Let me think a minute. Why don't you come back at 1:30 anyway, and you might as well bring your families along. You'll need somebody to sit with while you watch the show."

"Seriously? All of them?" I asked.

"Consider it a bonus for a group of hard working young men. Oh, like William pointed out, you will need to stick around afterwards to pick up before the night performance. I think I can still squeeze some work out of you."

Our feet took us flying home that day. We were taking our families to the circus. All the way home we talked about how great we were and how our families were going to be surprised. I remember seeing Tillie clapping her fingertips together as we all hollered in excitement. She was as happy as we were.

Reporting to the ticket booth at 1:30 with our families was the best day of our young lives. Father and Uncle Lyle looked especially proud of us as we were all escorted to a special section under the big top. Tillie was there to greet us, snake and all. Mother didn't like it and kept trying to protect Sister, but Sister was fascinated and loved it when Tillie let her pet Linus' head.

Much to our surprise, our grandmother reached her hand

right out and stroked Linus' long back. "Hello, darling. Aren't you beautiful," she said.

I had never seen Aunt Catherine get that excited. She couldn't stop talking. "We are so grateful to be here today. It's so generous of you and your father. We couldn't be more pleased, and not only to see the circus, but we're so thankful our boys got to work here."

Father added, "Yes, we're all pleasantly surprised at what a good experience this has been for the boys. I think it's put some hair on their chests, if you know what I mean."

"The pleasure has been all ours. They're hard workers and have become good friends." Tillie paused, "You'll have to excuse me. I wish I could stay and chat longer, but I think something has flown into my eye. I better go and tend to it," she said and quickly turned away.

Mother and Aunt Catherine glanced at each other and we all took our seats.

The circus began with Mr. Santamaria dressed in his suit proclaiming, "Here before your very eyes, you will see elephants from far off India with lovely ladies riding upon their backs." And with that, in walked the elephants, pausing in the middle ring, resting their front feet on each other making a mountain range of elephants. The tigers, clowns and acrobats drew our attention from one ring to another. Tillie strutted around between acts with Linus, who I believe even winked at us when he passed our area. It went by way too fast and before we knew it, we were shoveling poop again, but it was the most satisfying poop shoveling ever.

CHAPTER 20

Farewell Party

By Sunday, Poop Hill was more like Poop Volcano. You could almost see the fumes spewing from it. It was disgusting, but it would make great fertilizer. Smithy said that fertilizer was like a good friend – you don't want to be without it even though at times it can stink something awful.

Our cleanup done, it was time for our last glass of lemonade with Tillie. We ran up to her door and knocked, but she wasn't there. Instead there was a note telling us how sorry she was not to say goodbye in person, but something had come up. We should go to her dad's trailer for our long-awaited pay day.

Mr. Santamaria greeted us and the other hired hands with a handful of papers marked with our names on them. Beside him there was a long table covered with a linen table cloth, upon which sat a cake pan elevated on a pedestal. We figured he was going to give us a farewell dessert or something.

He began, "A final lesson is in order – a little something to leave you with before you go back to your everyday lives, which, by the way, will never be the same. Working at the circus changes a person. It opens up your minds to possibilities that you never even imagined. It allows you to see close up the magic behind the performance, which is largely a lot of hard work by a lot of dedicated people. And then you have the privilege of watching faces transform from frowns to smiles as people step into the big top. You get to witness the rebirth of joy and hope in people, especially in times such as these when hope is hard to find and want is the norm. The Depression doesn't exist at the circus – only elation."

I whispered to Tommy, "I will be a magician someday. You wait and see. Working here has made me want it more than ever."

He handed us each our paper. It was ordinary except for the fancy printing of our names.

"Now, one by one pass by the table and drop your papers inside of the cake pan," he said. Then he knocked on his trailer door, "I need my assistant please."

Tillie emerged from the trailer with a small, lit torch and asked, "Is it time to make the cake?"

"Most assuredly," her father replied.

She lowered the torch into the cake pan and lit the papers. Mr. Santamaria covered the pan with its lid as the papers blazed.

"There you go," he said. "A paycheck is like that. You work hard for it; and then, poof, it goes up in flames before you know it. It still is a reward, but the real reward is the feeling you get from working hard. That's the lasting fruit of your labor."

With that he took the cover off of the cake pan and it was full of dollar bills. He gave us nine each.

"Wow! That's the best magic trick ever," I said as I tried to peak around the cake pan to figure it out. "How'd you do that?"

"A magician never reveals his tricks," said Mr. Santamaria.

Tommy looked at me and said, "Yeah, you've got some work to do, Artie."

Before this, I felt rich if I had two nickels. I never actually had even one dollar of my own – now I was staring at nine of them in my hand.

Bucky kept muttering, "Hello, Mr. President, it's nice to see you – and you – and you – and you – and, of course, you, Mr. President."

I looked up at Mr. Santamaria. I had never met anyone quite like him. "Do you think one day I could do magic like you do?"

"Of course you could, and so much more. Keep working hard like you did for us, and you'll do fine in this world. And don't forget to look for the magic in all of what life has for you."

It was hard to say goodbye, especially to Tillie; but it was time. Mr. Santamaria's parting words were ringing in my ears as we walked home. As we neared the edge of the property, I looked back and there was Tillie, her dad's arm around her shoulders, waving Linus's tail at us. One last wave from us and we said goodbye to our career as circus folk and goodbye to a good friend.

That night our dinner table looked different. Grandmother, Mom and Aunt Catherine had set up three courses with rings of peas around them. Mom tried hard to get Dad to introduce the courses, but ended up doing it herself. "Ladies and Gentlemen, in this ring see the mashed potatoes, gravy perched alongside ready to magically turn what is white into a creamy brown. And in this ring – be astounded by peas and carrots as they swirl around the bowl. Ring Number Three will leave you satisfied as formerly live chickens dance around your taste buds."

Yes, Mom was strange, but she made life fun. Our dinner conversation was lively as we recounted our days at the circus.

I practiced my magic tricks from my kit before going to bed. I was getting smoother, but I knew these were kid's tricks. I was a long way from the big time.

I looked forward to sleeping in after getting up and working for 11 days straight. There was still a lot of summer ahead of us, and our parents kept mentioning that they weren't quite sure how we were going to fill it. Why do parents feel it is always necessary to have time used well? I guess I'll never figure that one out. It's just how it is.

CHAPTER 21

Houdini

It was barely light out and Grandfather was sitting in the kitchen drinking his coffee and eating toast and jam when Bucky, Tommy and I stumbled to the table. He said, "Your internal clock must be stuck on circus time. There's no poop around here for you to scoop today. You may as well go back to bed."

"Hey," Bucky said. "The poop wasn't my job. I'm used to eating early now, like the animals at the circus, I guess." And with that we each sat down and gobbled up three pieces of bread with jam, a banana and a bowl of corn flakes.

Grandfather stared at us and scratched his head as we inhaled our breakfast. "You boys are going to need something to do to burn off all that food. Make sure you stay out of trouble."

Bucky, Tommy and I sat and stared at each other.

"Any ideas?" Bucky asked.

"We could get away with going over to the harbor and watching the boats come in. Especially if we take our fishing poles and try to bring home dinner," Tommy suggested as he pulled the peel down on another banana.

"Nah, that's too iffy. What if we don't catch anything? Then we'd have to tote our poles around all day for nothing," I said.

"Well, if we don't come up with something fast, Mom will."

Right on cue, Mother entered the room. "Good morning, boys. And aren't you up early this morning?" she said as she danced around the kitchen. I liked seeing her happy and humming a tune as she ground beans for a fresh pot of coffee. By the looks of things, she had been up a while.

It was Monday; that meant it was washday. She already had sheets on the clothesline blowing in the breeze. If we didn't get out soon…..

"How about helping me out with Louise today? She missed you fellows while you've been working at the circus."

"I can't today," Bucky replied. "I'm pretty sure I have to do something for my dad." Quickly Bucky was out the door leaving Tommy and me on our own.

"We were thinking about heading down to the water and doing a little fishing," Tommy said in desperation.

"Perfect, you can take Louise with you. She loves watching the boats and the seagulls. Go get your bed made and brush your teeth. Then you can get your fishing gear together. I'll have Louise ready for you when you're finished."

Walking up the steps to our room and out of Mother's sight, I took the opportunity to punch Tommy right in the shoulder. "Now look what you've done."

"Well, I didn't hear you coming up with anything. At least we don't have to hang around here all day and get stuck helping with the laundry and whatever else Mom comes up with."

I don't know why our mom referred to our fishing stuff as "gear." We had seen men with fishing gear – shiny rods with reels on them and tackle boxes full of lures and artificial bait. Now that was gear. We had old bamboo poles with some fishing line and a hook that would hardly hold a fish big enough to feed one person. The stuff we caught was what those other people used as bait, but we were always happy to go fishing.

Now, taking our little sister out for the day can be trying enough, but for some odd reason Mom had her wearing a dress and galoshes. Her hair was in pigtails with big red bows in them. She stood out like a sore thumb. It looked like she couldn't decide if she was going to Sunday School or going to dig clams.

"Mom, is that what she's wearing?"

"She insisted. She wanted to be fancy to go out with her brothers and thought the galoshes would be perfect in case she got too close to the water. It's hard to argue with that kind of logic."

We kept Sister in between us as we walked to the water. She had a tendency to disappear so we needed to keep her in view.

As we walked toward the water, we passed people putting up elaborate posters advertising a big show at the Hippodrome Theater. "Look, Tommy, Howard Thurston is bringing his magic show to town. There's got to be a way for us to see him."

"Nah, you know it's going to cost too much. Our parents would never let us spend any of our money to go."

"But look at him. His eyes are burning holes in my head. It's like he's calling my name. Besides, we each have nine dollars."

"Maybe you're right. I think I hear him saying – 'Artie, Artie. You will ask your father if you can come to my show. He will tell you that there is no way you're spending your money on that nonsense.'"

Tommy was always too practical, and unfortunately usually right. Our parents would call going to a show extravagant for sure. But all the way to town those posters kept taunting me.

It was still pretty early in the day, but by the time we got to the harbor most of the good fishing places had been taken. True fishermen wake up with the fishes, our grandfather would say. Of course, true fishermen don't go fishing with a little girl in a dress with bows in her hair, cradling a baby doll in her arms either, but oh well.

We lucked out as a man was leaving a prime spot right by a maple tree. We could tell already that it was going to be another hot one, and the shade would be welcome. "You stay right here under the tree. Play with your doll and watch the boats and birds. Don't even think about wandering off anywhere, Little Turkey," we told her in no uncertain terms.

In addition to calling Louise, Sister, she had earned the nickname "Little Turkey." She did tend to wander off, and our dad thought she reminded him of a little turkey gobbling and wandering about looking for something to eat. Today she seemed content to sit and watch the boats while holding her little doll, much to our relief.

"Maybe there are too many people here today," Tommy said, breaking a long silence. "I'll bet we've been here for hours, and we haven't had one nibble."

"We haven't been here for hours. Look, the sun isn't even directly over our heads yet. Be patient. Look at Sister, she's happy, so what's the hurry?"

Sister was happy playing under the tree. She had gathered up some small stones and shells and was arranging them around her doll. She hummed like our mom did when she was working around the house.

Tommy and I started reminiscing about the circus. I said, "I still can't believe we worked at a circus. It was great. And the magic cake pan was amazing. I wonder how Mr. Santamaria did that."

"It has to be a trick pan. How else could he have made those dollars out of paper? We'll have to get ourselves one of those someday. Too bad there wasn't one in your magic kit."

Tommy was getting more and more interested in magic, too. So much so that I was afraid that he wouldn't want to be my assistant any more, but it was too soon to worry about that yet. We still didn't even know how to do any real tricks. But, we discovered as we turned around, Sister did. She had disappeared.

"Oh, man, we're going to get killed. Louise, Louise," we yelled. But she was nowhere to be seen. She had disappeared into thin air and even left her doll behind. We looked up and down the shore and there was no sign of her.

We decided to split up and meet back at the tree. I ran as fast as I could around the water's edge and asked everyone if they had seen her, but no one had. Tommy went the other direction with the same results. We didn't dare go home without her – that was for sure. We picked up our poles and her doll and started to move away from the water into town. The harbor wasn't the nicest area. There were a lot of dockworkers moving crates around and trucks going in and out loading or unloading the ships' cargos. You had to be careful. Our parents had only recently started letting us go fishing down here.

As we were about to leave the area, we noticed a fishing boat having its catch unloaded onto a truck. There were several stray cats hanging around enjoying the smell of fresh fish and hoping for a handout.

We asked the workers if they had seen Louise and one said, "I wasn't paying any attention to anything except unloading the fish, but it's hard not to notice a little girl with big red bows in her hair chasing cats all over the place. We had to shoo her away so she wouldn't get run over."

"That sure sounds like her. Do you know where she went?"

"Haven't the slightest idea. You better get out of here, too, before you get yourselves in trouble."

117

We decided to try to pet or even get close to the cats. Maybe we could get a clue to help us find Sister, but they wouldn't have it and ran away.

"Those are feral cats, kid. They're not going to let you get anywhere near them," said an older man who was leaning against the truck.

"Did you see a little girl chasing after any of these this morning?" I asked.

"As a matter of fact, I did. A cute little thing with red bows in her hair. She belong to you?"

"Yes sir, we were fishing and keeping an eye on her for our mother."

"Well, I'd say by looking at your empty poles and that baby doll you're toting around, that you haven't been all too good at either one of those jobs this morning, have you?"

"No, sir, we haven't. No fish biting and that little sister of ours can disappear quicker than Houdini."

"Houdini, huh? Well, I remember seeing Houdini do a show right here in Baltimore years ago. The difference between him and your sister is he always reappeared. Let's hope your sister does, too. I've seen these here cats coming and going toward that big old dumpster over there. You may want to see if your sister followed any of them that way."

We did find a mother cat with two kittens sucking on her, but no sign of Sister. This was the kind of thing that our sister couldn't resist. We tried to get close to the mother, but noises came out of her that sounded meaner than a circus cat.

I asked Tommy, "Have you ever known any cat to only have two kittens? I mean, there are plenty more places for more kittens to latch on. I wonder if there are more around here somewhere."

We looked all over – under cardboard boxes and inside

old crates, around corners and even behind a man who was sleeping in the alley.

"This place stinks something terrible. I can't imagine Sister hanging around here too long. But I can imagine her taking off with a kitten if she could have gotten her hands on one," Tommy said.

Tommy was looking a little greenish.

"Are you okay, Tommy?"

"I don't know if it's the smell of this place, but my stomach is feeling horrible. I think I'm going to puke."

"Why do you throw up every time you get a little nervous?"

"I don't every time. And I'm not a little nervous. I'm a lot nervous. Our sister is missing," he said and then he vomited all over a pile of cardboard.

We didn't know what to do. We couldn't find any clues except for the fact that there were only two kittens, and that wasn't proving to be too helpful. We circled back around to the maple tree and found Sister's stone and shell design was half gone. "She's been here. I know it," Tommy said.

After searching for a long time, we couldn't think of anything else to do except go home and get more help. We were going to have to tell our parents that not only did we not catch any fish for dinner, but Sister got away from us, too. We were torn between running home to get help fast and not wanting to get there at all, but we decided running home was the only option. We needed help.

About halfway home Tommy stopped and held his stomach. He was panting hard and I think he was starting to cry. Then he puked all over the sidewalk.

"We can't stop now, Tommy. Wipe yourself down and keep going."

We rounded the corner of the long line of row houses where

our grandparents lived, still running. All we could hope for was that our dad wasn't home yet. Mom would be upset but keep her wits about her. Dad, on the other hand, would be livid. We had lost a lot of things in our short lifetimes and gotten in plenty of trouble for it, but we couldn't even imagine what the punishment would be for losing our sister.

Seeing Grandmother sitting on the front stoop doing her needlepoint was a welcome sight. She was the best one to go to in times of trouble. She had softened the blow of discipline for us many a time, but we didn't expect to get off the hook with this one. "Hello there, boys. You sure seem in a hurry. Sit down and tell me about your day."

"There's no time. We need help. Sister," I said, "Sister has gone Little Turkey on us. We can't find her anywhere!"

"I'm not sure what you're talking about or what exactly little turkey means, but one thing is clear, you boys are overheated and need a drink of water. Tommy, you look horrible."

"Grandmother, Sister is missing. Didn't you hear what we said?"

"Now, now. I know my hearing is a little off, but what exactly is your sister missing?"

"She is not missing anything. She is missing," Tommy pleaded. "Get Mother please!"

She took us inside, poured us some water and went out back to get our mother. Poor Mom, she had no idea what news she was about to hear. We watched out the window and waited for Mom's reaction. She continued taking the sheets off the line like usual. Tommy and I sat in silent confusion and downed our water.

"This must be what death row feels like," Tommy said.

"Grandmother isn't hearing us right. We have to do something," I said as Tommy ran to the kitchen sink and threw up again.

Finally, after what seemed like an eternity but must have been about three minutes, Grandmother walked in, followed by Mother with a basket of clothes under her arm.

"Did Grandmother tell you Sister is missing?" I asked as I sprung to my feet.

"Yes, she did mention something to that effect."

"I can't believe you took the time to take the clothes down, Mom. What are we going to do? Sister could be anywhere."

"She could be, but she isn't. About two hours ago, she showed up here all sweaty and smelling like fish, carrying a little kitten. She told me that while you two were fishing and talking, she went to pet a kitty, and when she brought it back to show you, you were clean gone. The poor thing. She was very upset. But isn't she the clever one to be able to find her way home all by herself. Now, as for you two…."

I thought that I would like to clever Sister right upside the head. "Mom, honest, it wasn't our fault. She's like Houdini."

"Listen, boys. We need to put this behind us as your Father is due home any minute. We won't speak of it again. I do like the name Houdini though. I think that's the perfect name for our new kitten."

As far as we could tell, our father was never told about any of this. The fact that Tommy and I had our death sentence suspended helped us deal with Sister escaping her punishment and being rewarded with a new kitten.

Mom and Aunt Catherine managed to quickly put together a nice dinner. Dad was disappointed that we weren't having fish, but distracted by watching Louise play with Houdini. "How did you come up with that name?" he asked.

"Oh, it seemed to fit," Mother said and sent us outside to play.

We played tag and hide-and-go-seek until it was nearly dark. We even ran slowly so that Sister could have a chance to catch us. If we didn't want her to tell Dad how she got Houdini, we would have to go out of our way to keep her happy for weeks.

As soon as the fireflies started flickering, our games shifted to firefly hunting. Grandmother came to the back door with a jar for each of us and the chase was on. Sister managed to squish a few with the lid of her jar, but she was getting better and better about that. All of us boys would fill our jars with enough to use for war paint. We smeared the fireflies on our faces and arms and went around like wild Indians, glowing in the night. We would let the rest go, but Sister always brought hers in for a nightlight.

Teeth brushed and ready for bed, we told Bucky and the gang about our fishing adventures. They couldn't believe that we were alive to tell the story.

CHAPTER 22

Hold on to Your Dream

Father was on the late shift now, so he was around more in the morning. Once in a while we would wake up to a visitor – someone who Dad had picked up from the train station late and needed a place to sleep. This morning when we found a total stranger sleeping on our couch, it was no surprise to us. The moms were fixing eggs and grits in the kitchen, and Dad was pouring coffee when we kids exploded down the stairs with our usual grand entrance. After our guest joined us and introductions were made, we sat quietly and ate our breakfast while the grown-ups talked.

Mr. Pack had come in on the 11:45 train last night, and Dad had been dispatched to pick him up. He was looking to get a room someplace cheap for the night; but after he and Dad talked in the cab, it was decided that our couch would do fine. He was an artist, a painter. He had been commissioned to come to town and paint a mural in the Hippodrome Theater, which wasn't too far from where we were living with our grandparents.

He had several bags with him, mostly full of paints and brushes. After breakfast, he showed us all of his supplies. I had never seen so many colors in my life. We all hit it off right away. Dad and Mom convinced him that he should come back and have dinner with us that night. Dinner turned into another night on our couch, for which he seemed grateful.

Morning was never my favorite time of day, even in the summer, until today. Usually I make my bed and do other chores – the stuff you have to finish to get to the stuff you want to do, but not today. Little did I know those many weeks ago, that the same taxicab company that had gotten me in big trouble would bring this man to our doorstep and change my life forever.

Mr. Pack had gotten permission from my parents to take me with him to work that day. I wasn't too excited about watching somebody paint, but there was something about Mr. Pack that made me want to be around him. He had a way of ruffling my hair and patting me on the shoulder that made me comfortable with him as if I had known him all my life.

I had been to a movie theater before, but had never been in a theater where live people perform. I was surprised at how big and fancy it was. Mr. Pack was doing a mural of a scene from Ancient Greece and thought he would be able to finish it in a couple of days. He painted a picture as fast as Tommy and I could paint the side of our shed – and better, too. According to Dad, Tommy and I left streaks when we painted so he made us apply a second coat; but Mr. Pack worked his way across that wall like nothing I had ever seen before.

It was amazing that he could paint and talk to me at the same time. He was full of interesting stories about Chicago and his family, but after a while my mind was starting to wander. My father had always said that the mind could only absorb what the posterior could endure, and my endurance was about up when Mr. Pack announced that it was lunchtime and gave me some brushes to go wash out with him.

"Artie, your father tells me that you are interested in show biz. Ever thought about acting?"

"No, not that kind of show biz. I want to be a magician."

"Have you ever seen a magician before?"

"Oh, yeah, of course. I saw some tricks done when I worked at the circus, and there's a man in our old neighborhood who has been doing tricks for us kids ever since I can remember."

"You've never been to a professional magic show then, so you've never seen a master magician."

"What is a master magician?" I asked.

"A master magician is one who has such formidable skills that he is indeed an artist. His performance suspends your disbelief in the illusions he performs."

"Have you seen one of those, Mr. Pack?"

"Yes, I've seen quite a few magicians in my day. Once I even saw Harry Houdini. Now Houdini is mainly known as an escape artist, but he was also a fine magician. Let me tell you, when he performed, it was magical."

"Wow, Houdini. We named our cat after him. I'd love to have seen him, but I'm pretty sure that he's dead now."

"Yes, he is. I know a magician who knew him well. This magician is by far the most amazing magician I have ever seen. He is a master magician. Would you believe he is performing here this very night?"

"You mean Howard Thurston, don't you? I've seen his posters all over town. I would give my eye teeth to see him."

"I think you should hold on to those, Artie," Mr. Pack said with a laugh.

My mind began to wander. This was the best thing I had ever heard – I was talking to a man who actually knows Howard Thurston! I kept thinking about what it would be like to meet him and see him perform. Then I thought about the day when I would be the master magician and my face would be plastered on posters all over town. I wondered if Tommy would be satisfied being behind the scenes. Then I heard my name.

"Artie. Artie. Would you?"

"Would I what?"

"I'm not sure where you went just now, but you were far from here. I'll bet you were on a stage somewhere in that head of yours. I asked if you would like to go back stage and meet Mr. Thurston."

"Would I? That would be a dream come true."

After lunch Mr. Pack parked me right outside of the dressing room doors so when Thurston, the Magician, came by I wouldn't miss him.

There were enough posters around town that I knew what Thurston looked like. Every time I walked by one, his dark eyes pierced my soul as they emerged from the frame of his wavy dark hair. But how would a magician look in person and how would he act when he wasn't doing magic? Or did he always do magic tricks. Was that his whole life? Surely he wouldn't always wear a cape or a fancy suit, but that was the image that kept coming to mind. Would he be wearing a silk top hat or at least have one tucked under his arm, like the one that I got from Miss Spencer?

I was not at all prepared for what the backstage area was like. There were a lot of people bustling around and animals in cages being wheeled past me. I had memorized those eyes from the poster and kept alert in case I spied them. It was like I wasn't even there. No one noticed me, but there was energy here, energy like I had never felt before.

The strangest part about it all was that I didn't mind sitting and waiting and watching what was going on. Usually I can't stand waiting for anything, but this place was fascinating. Eventually a young man knocked on one of the doors and said, "Mr. T, your silks are ready for inspection." The door opened and there stood a man who wasn't a lot taller than I was. His hair was nicely groomed. He wore an undershirt, and his suspenders hung from the waist of his pants.

I thought that he must be another member of the crew until he looked over at me with those eyes that had beckoned me from the posters. He nodded as he passed and followed the other man down the corridor. I could hardly breathe. A real master magician had nodded his head at me. Somehow with that small nod of the head I was paralyzed. I could not speak or move and my mind shut down. I sat and stared with my mouth, I am sure, hanging open.

After an hour or so, this ordinary looking man with the extraordinary eyes reappeared. He leaned down and with one hand he closed my mouth while the other hand reached behind my ear and produced a coin, which he placed in my hand. "Good afternoon, young man. You're a little early to see the show."

There was a quality to his voice that in itself was magic. When those eyes looked at me and I heard that voice, I was transformed. I managed to explain all about Mr. Pack and how I ended up coming down here with him and how, unfortunately, I wouldn't be able to stay for the show.

"Magicians make the impossible possible," he began. "Like pulling a coin out from behind your ear. I wonder how long that had been waiting there to be discovered," he said as he reached his hand out and pulled another coin from the other ear. He clasped that coin in his hand and had me blow on it. He slowly opened his hand, one finger at a time, to reveal the coin had disappeared. Then he removed a deck of cards from his pocket and proceeded to amaze me with his slight-of-hand. He waved a card in the air and it disappeared only to reappear with the next wave of his hand.

"I know Mr. Pack," he continued as he balanced the deck of cards between his thumb and fingers and cut the deck of cards with one hand without blinking an eye. "He thinks that you need to see this show tonight. If you had but one coin, you could gain admission."

My mouth dropped open again as he took the coin from my hand and told me that there would be seats for me and for Mr. Pack front row center. "It will be my pleasure to see you both this evening," he said with a flourish. Right before he disappeared into his dressing room, he turned, gave me a wink and flipped the coin to me.

At that point I was sure nothing could beat my encounter with Howard Thurston. I was dazzled by his every move and I hung on his every word – "It will be my pleasure to see you this evening." His pleasure! Mr. Pack had told me that Mr. Thurston was a fine gentleman and extremely kind, but I had not dared to hope that he would speak to me, much less invite me to see his show.

Mr. Pack was as thrilled to see the show as I was and made sure that we were in our seats as early as possible so as not to miss a thing. When a John Philip Sousa march began and the lights dimmed, I felt like electricity was going through my entire body. The curtain went up and there he was. He was surrounded by fanfare like I had never seen or imagined – even more than was used at the circus.

He did one illusion after another, working with silks, ropes and shiny silver hoops. Then, the upbeat music changed to a more mysterious sound. The lights dimmed and from his pocket he produced a single deck of cards. How one man could entertain such a large room with a deck of cards was amazing.

For the finale, he proceeded to sail cards one by one all over the room, even up to the balcony. The audience clamored to catch one of these special souvenirs. I was one of the lucky ones. I was thrilled to discover that this wasn't a regular playing card. It had his picture on it. This day sealed it for me. My fascination with magic was transformed into a true pursuit of being a magician.

The evening passed much too quickly, and before I knew it I was home with my coin and my card. Tommy was so jealous he would barely talk to me; but he chalked it up to the fact that I was the oldest, and this was one of the unfair rewards that went along with that.

Breakfast was a sad occasion, as we had to say goodbye to Mr. Pack. "It's been such a pleasure to stay here with you good people," he said. "I don't know how I could ever repay you for your hospitality, but if you ever get to Chicago, you'll have a warm bed and meal waiting for you."

With that he gave Grandmother a gift that was wrapped in white paper and tied up with twine. She was so excited that she didn't seem to know what to do. All of us kids cried out for her to open it, and she managed to compose herself enough to do so. "Land sakes, sir, you surely didn't have to get me a gift," she said as she carefully unwrapped the present and folded the wrapping paper.

"I didn't exactly get you a gift," he responded.

As the paper fell to the floor we gasped as a beautiful picture of the front of our grandparents' home was revealed. He hadn't missed a detail. There were seven steps flanked by iron railings rising up to the solid oak door. The weathered doorknocker looked as if I could reach out and touch it. Sitting by the bottom step was the cast iron foot scraper, and it even had dirt on it. Grandmother's stool that she liked to sit on while she watched the street go by, as she called it, had a basket of pussy willows leaning against it.

"I don't know what to say," she managed to squeak out. "It's beautiful. Thank you. Thank you very much." She hugged him goodbye and as she pulled away I noticed a place on his shirt that was freshly stained by her tears.

After insisting that it was nothing, he extended his hand to each of us kids and we offered our farewells.

"Artie," he said, "can you give me a hand carrying my things to your dad's taxi?"

I picked up his suitcase and he carried his art supplies to the car. I hated to see him leave. I was at a loss for words to tell him how much I appreciated all he did for me, and then all the sudden they started gushing out. "Thank you for taking me to work with you yesterday. I can't believe that you actually know Mr. Thurston. It was the neatest thing ever seeing his show and sitting backstage watching everything. Do you think I could ever be a magician? I mean, I don't know how to do any tricks other than the ones in my magic kit, and they are more like a kid's toys. I don't know how to learn any either. I guess you have to start somewhere though, where I'm not sure of, but…"

"If it's meant to be, it'll happen," he said with a nice even tone. "Keep watching for those opportunities to learn and observe. Like yesterday, they turn up when you least expect them," he said as he put his bags in the trunk. "And, don't ever give up on your dream. Who knows what the future holds?" After one more tussle of my hair, he and my dad climbed into the cab and disappeared from view.

CHAPTER 23

The Smell of Home

It was hard to think about anything except magic; but as Mom said, until I could wave a magic wand and get my chores done, I'd have to do them the old-fashioned way.

With our beds made and rooms cleaned, we reported to our mothers for further orders.

"It seems that we don't have much to do today, so let's have an outing. We could use a little distraction from thinking about Mr. Pack and magic."

As we walked downtown with our moms, we looked like a pathetic parade zigzagging down the street. Mom and Aunt Catherine had to keep counting heads so as not to lose any of us, especially Sister. They were enjoying the fact that we didn't know what was going on.

"Where are we going?" we pleaded. The mothers smiled and said we'd find out soon enough.

"I know – we're going shopping. Wait, maybe we're going to a restaurant," Bucky guessed.

"Nah," I replied. "We can't afford a restaurant."

"Well, we can," Leroy said in a nasty tone.

131

"That's enough," Aunt Catherine said with authority.

The roads in the city were becoming more and more familiar. We had roller-skated along these roads a lot. I knew we were going towards the train station, but I couldn't figure out what was happening. "Please, Mom, tell us. What are we doing?"

"Here I thought you boys liked a mystery, but you can't stand it, can you? You're going to have to wait and see," Mom said as she led us into the train station. She and Aunt Catherine walked right up to the ticket window with us following behind like a family of quail. "We'd like tickets to Ferndale, please, two adults and seven children."

"Ferndale? We're going back to our old neighborhood?"

"That's right, just for a visit. We thought it might be fun to see what's been going on since we moved away."

Sister threw her hands over her ears at the sound of the train screeching to a halt. "All aboard," the conductor yelled.

It was only a twenty-minute trip, but the steady beat of the train down the tracks was enough to put Sister to sleep. We laughed at her as we watched her eyes droop and then suddenly pop open. Her head bobbed and jerked upright over and over, and then her eyes closed and she fell over onto Mom's lap sound asleep.

We boys were chattering even louder than the train. The excitement rose with every stop until at last the conductor said, "Next stop, Ferndale."

Mother got off first. She had a strange look on her face as we all jumped off the train steps. "I don't know if every place has its own smell, but if there is a smell that could be labeled 'home,' to me, this is it."

She and Aunt Catherine didn't seem to want to move. "How long are our moms going to stand there smelling?" Leroy whispered.

I shrugged my shoulders. I had never seen Mom like this.

"I don't know if it's freshly cut grass or Mr. Cox's big old pine trees, but I love that aroma," Mother said with a smile. "I could drink this fragrance in the rest of my life and it would be okay with me."

Finally, I got up the nerve to interrupt. "Mom, do you think that you and Aunt Catherine have smelled enough?"

The moms laughed and we all strolled down the street. "How long has it been now since we lived here, Mom?" Tommy asked.

"It's only been a few months."

"Seems longer, seems like years," I said. I couldn't wait to see what our house looked like. Ours was the third one on the right. The first one had been emptied out even before we moved, and it still looked empty to me. A married couple from France had lived next door, but that house looked empty now, too. The grass was tall and the bushes by the front door almost blocked the walkway.

"This place looks like a ghost town," William stated. "I don't think anybody lives in most of these houses. Yours looks empty, don't you think?"

Mom answered, "Yes, it sure does. Looks like nobody's been in it since we left. It's heartbreaking to see our home sitting vacant."

"Why don't we move in if nobody lives there?" asked Louise.

"It doesn't work that way, Sister," I said.

"It does give us the chance to peek in the windows," Tommy said.

We were starting to go around to the backyard when a familiar voice came from across the street, "Hey, Tommy, what ya doing around here?"

"Hey, Paul," Tommy yelled back. "We're just visiting."

"Well come on over. I'll tell my mom you're all here."

I liked Mrs. Cox a lot. She always had cookies for us to eat and didn't mind us hanging around too much. When she appeared at their front door wiping her hands on her apron, it was like we had never moved away.

Their kitchen was warm and welcoming. There was a bird chattering in a cage in the corner, but we drowned him out with all our voices. Mrs. Cox wasn't quite used to this amount of kids in her kitchen and soon gave Paul a plate of cookies and handed Tommy a pitcher of lemonade. We were banished to the backyard. We didn't mind being outside, especially here. It felt like home.

Paul was like an only child. She had two brothers, but they were over ten years older than her. Since we moved away, she was around grown-ups all the time, she told us. There were never any ball games in the vacant lot next door. So many people had moved to find work or live with relatives.

"Things are picking up though," William said. "Our dad is working now and maybe we won't have to live with the grandparents too much longer."

"It must be boring for you guys living in the city," Paul said.

"Nah," said Tommy. "It's been one adventure after another."

We filled her in on our exploits. Even Louise had a story to tell about her adventure at the harbor and her new cat Houdini.

Bucky interrupted, "Enough of this chitter-chatter – let's play marbles or something."

We ran to the field next door and played a game of tag while the ladies stayed in the kitchen playing pinochle and catching up with each other over tea. Paul told us that her dad and her brother, Ernie, were both working at the chemical plant. Things were going well for the Cox family.

Time passed way too quickly; and before we knew it, we were returning to the city.

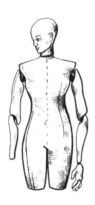

CHAPTER 24

Lumps, Bumps and Triumphs

Times were improving. Uncle Lyle and Aunt Catherine were planning to move back to Ferndale. Uncle Lyle would continue his work as a carpenter/handy man and could come into town on the train when necessary. With employment shaping up, Tommy and I were hopeful that we would be able to return home, too.

Before we knew it, Uncle Lyle and Aunt Catherine packed up their things, along with the boys, and piled into Grandfather's truck. They were moving back to Ferndale. Their new home was across the tracks from our old one, but still it made me crazy to think they were going back and we could not. Two trips later, they were gone. The house was so quiet. Tommy and I didn't know what to do with ourselves. It's a big change going from six boys to two boys, not to mention one little sister.

We strapped on our roller skates. The streets were busy with mothers shopping and kids like us looking for something to do. Tommy and I decided to race each other to the Hippodrome for fun.

I yelled, "On your mark, get set, go." Off we went, dodging in and out of people and risking it all for the glory of the win. Tommy won easily.

"I demand a re-match. The first one home will be the World Champion Skater and the last will have to do the dinner dishes with only Sister to help."

"That's not exactly fair since I won already; but since I know I'll win again, let's do it," Tommy said.

We tore down the street and around corners. We were good. We could practically fly on those skates – forwards and backwards. Down the final stretch, Tommy was in the lead. People were jumping out of our way and yelling at us as we passed them. I gave it all I had but could not catch him. What I did catch, however, was a car door that opened exactly at the wrong time. Thankfully, the window was down so that when I hit it at full speed, I flipped through it and fell flat on my back on the pavement.

The last thing I remembered hearing was Tommy yelling, "I'm winning! Have fun doing dishes."

I don't know how long I was out, but I could tell by Mother's face that she was concerned. She had that look that said – I want to wring your neck as soon as I know you're okay. The only bright side was that I did get out of the dishes that night. My head had a huge lump on it the size of Montana, and my arms and back were all scraped up. I had to keep ice on my head and take it easy for the rest of the night.

Twice in the night I threw up. It was weird because my stomach didn't hurt at all. Grandmother sat with me all night long. She kept looking at my eyes and taking my temperature. She would wake me up out of a sound sleep and then apologize for it. I had never seen her so worried.

The next day I had a headache like I had never had before. The doctor even came and looked at me. He pulled my eyelids down and shined a light in my eyes. He made me follow his finger from side to side. He listened to me breathing and hit my knees and elbows with a little rubber hammer. I even had to walk across the room on my heels with my arms held out to the side and then stand on one foot and then the other. Walking was hard to do. I would walk a little and then lose my balance. I figured I must be dying or something because I heard him whispering to my parents and grandparents after he examined me.

"Rest, you need to rest. You have a concussion, but you'll be fine," said my mother when she checked in on me. Her face had a less worried look.

My father was somewhat less gentle. "What on earth were you and your knucklehead brother thinking, racing around the city like that? You might have been killed or, God forbid, hurt somebody else. With a brain as small as yours, you ought not risk having it splat all over the pavement."

Tommy came in and Dad yelled at us together for a while. After Dad left, Tommy said he had heard whispering earlier, too. "It has to be bad. I hope you don't die."

"Me, too." I didn't think I was going to die, but what did I know. I did figure that my parents wouldn't tell me if I was dying. That's just how they were.

The hot, still, summer air penetrated my room and made my stomach and head feel even worse. Grandmother brought me some saltines and ginger ale. Her cool hand pushing the hair back off my forehead felt good. She sat with me a long time and read to me while I ate. If there are angels, I bet they're a lot like my grandmother.

The next morning the lump on my head was down, but I

still felt like I had been hit by a truck. Everything hurt. The smell of food wafting up the stairs helped encourage me out of bed though, and I reported for breakfast as usual. If my father yelling at me hadn't made me doubt the thought of my impending death, the hunger pains did.

"Well, well," Mother said, "look who made it down the stairs for breakfast. How are you feeling this morning?"

"Better, I guess. It feels like I got beat up. Even my hair hurts."

"You're going to be fine," she said. And I believed her.

Tommy and Sister were already down eating their breakfast. Grandfather had gone off to hawk vegetables and Father had a meeting with his boss.

"Grandmother and I were planning on taking you kids to buy shoes today. We'll at least get some for you and Sister. Tommy, you can probably fit in Artie's old shoes."

"Are you feeling up to going out for a while, Artie?" Grandmother asked as I finished my breakfast.

"I think so. Breakfast tastes good and I don't feel like I'm going to puke anymore."

Mother replied, "I guess that's all I can ask for."

Tommy and I said we were ready to go, but Mother disagreed.

"You need to wash your feet," Mother said.

"You mean, Artie, right? I'm not getting shoes," Tommy said.

"You need to wash yours, too, Thomas, just in case. It won't hurt you a bit."

Grandmother added, "It would not do at all to have a salesman pass out from the smell of stinky boy feet, and he should not have to stuff a big toe back in a sock to try a shoe on you."

138

"Yes, make sure you wear socks with no holes," Mother said.

Grandmother and Mother looked so put together with their hats and gloves on as we all walked to the shopping district. Sister, of course, did as well.

Mother said, "You two boys look like street urchins."

"At least we're street urchins with clean socks," I said.

"With no holes in them, too," Tommy added.

Sister would be starting school this year. She was giggling all over the store while trying on shoes. She wanted to try on all of them. Mother decided that a pair of Mary Janes would do. For Tommy and me, a shoe was a shoe. We were anxious to make the purchase and get out of there.

Sister insisted on wearing her new shoes out of the store. Mother insisted that I carry mine. Tommy washed his feet for nothing.

Grandmother said, "It's awfully hot out today. What do you say we take in a matinee since we're close to the theater?"

"That sounds great. I'm pretty hot and my head still hurts a little," I said as I touched my head gently feeling for the remains of the bump.

"I imagine a movie will do you a world of good," Mother said with a chuckle.

When Tommy and I saw the marquee – Tarzan and His Mate with Johnny Weissmuller – we went wild. Suddenly I didn't notice if my head hurt or not.

This was a huge treat. Sitting in a comfy chair, munching on candy and watching a movie – it doesn't get much better than that.

As we walked home after the movie, Tommy and I pounded our chests and did our best Tarzan yells.

When we walked into the house, Sister did an impression of

Cheetah, Tarzan's pet chimp, that was so good Father came in to check it out.

"Is this my family or a troop of monkeys?"

"It's me, Father. I made that noise. We went to see Tarzan. Cheetah is my favorite," Sister said.

"I think you'd be his favorite, too, Louise. You sound like him. Now, you children go upstairs and let your mother and I talk.

I was still a little tired from the accident, so going upstairs for a while sounded good.

That night after we finished our dinner, Sister asked, "May I please be excused from the table?"

"Me, too," Tommy and I added.

"No, you may not," said Father.

"Are we in trouble?" I asked.

"What do you think? Did you do something wrong?"

"Not that I know of," Tommy answered.

"There is the skating accident. I haven't gotten punished for that yet."

"I never do anything wrong," said Louise.

"I don't know about that," said Father, "but this is not about anybody being in trouble. This is about the future – particularly about school starting again."

"Summer can't be over already," I groaned.

"I don't want to go to a new school," Tommy said.

"I can't wait to go to school," Louise chirped.

"You're all getting ahead of me. Summer is not over yet, though it will be before we know it. And who said anything about going to a new school?"

"We can't take the train every day to our old one. So, what choice do we have?" I asked.

Father stood up. "Listen, you will go to school where I say you will go. Is that clear? And, if I say we can move back to our old home in Ferndale and you have to go to your old school, well then that's exactly what you'll do."

"Really? You're not messing with us?" I asked, looking at Mother.

"Really," Mother said.

Tommy and I burst out of our seats yelling and screaming and doing Tarzan yells until Mother reminded us that we were at the table.

"Nothing wrong with a little celebrating. Good news is good news and worth making some noise about, even if it we are at the table. Though the timing of this particular celebration right after a Tarzan film could have been better," Grandmother said.

Sister jumped up and ran from the table. She returned with Houdini in her arms. "What about him? Can he come, too?"

"Of course he can," Father said. "As long as you take care of him"

"And Maggie. What about Maggie?" I asked.

"Maybe your grandparents would like to keep Maggie," Father said.

Grandfather said, "Uh, no. I don't think so. She's Artie's and wherever Artie is – well, that's where Maggie should be also."

"Maggie's not as cute and compact as a kitten, but at least she doesn't have to be fed. If there's room on the truck she can come. If not, I guess you'll have to cut her in half and stick her in the truck bed piecemeal," Father said. "Then maybe you can finally do that magic trick you're always talking about."

"Now Arthur," Mother said. "She got here fine. She'll get

home fine, too."

Two days later Grandfather's truck made the trip to Ferndale to move our family back to our old house.

Grandmother cried as the truck was loaded. "I've loved having you children here. It's going to be way too quiet now for my liking."

"This is a good thing," Grandfather said. "Families do need each other, but it's best when they can be a family on their own."

Before we took our final load, Grandmother whispered in my ear, "You will always have a place here, both in our home and in my heart, no matter what. I'm here if you need me. I love you."

We each gave her one more hug and then we were off.

CHAPTER 25

Getting Back to Normal

As we pulled in our old driveway, we saw Paul and her dad sitting on their front porch. She waved and he nodded like no time had passed and we had returned from running an errand or something.

"They sure don't seem surprised to see us," I mentioned.

"They knew we were coming home," Mom said. "Remember our train visit? We were pretty sure about this then, and I told Mrs. Cox. I guess she let the cat out of the bag and told the family."

It was a hot morning and we sweated up a storm as we unloaded the truck and toted boxes into the house. Mother opened up all the windows, wiped the kitchen down and swept the front porch. Soon we had our few large belongings in place – the kitchen table and chairs, the corner hutch for Mom's good dishes, the sofa and rocking chair, the beds and, of course, Maggie.

Everything was the same. Tommy and I shared the same room. Sister had the room next door, and our parents were across the hall. Mr. Cox told us that a lot of our old friends had found their way back to the neighborhood, too. Life was returning to normal.

That afternoon, Father left for his shift driving a taxi. Tommy, Sister and I helped Mom finish organizing the house.

"I can't wait to put together a game of marbles," Tommy said.

"Me, too. Maybe Bucky and the guys can come over on Saturday and we'll get a game going."

Mother overheard us and said, "You don't have to wait until Saturday. Aunt Catherine is bringing dinner for us tonight. Uncle Lyle and the boys are coming as well. You might manage to get a game in before your father gets home for dinner – that is if we get our work done."

At 4:30, Bucky and his family arrived. Aunt Catherine and Uncle Lyle brought enough food to feed an army, according to Mom. William, Bucky, Leroy and Edgar were carrying their roller skates.

As we boys strapped on our skates, Sister showed up and Mom made us take her with us. The seven of us happily skated along the familiar streets. We went up the hill, past the church, all the way to the school. Sister and Edgar even kept up. We sat down at the picnic benches and rested.

William said, "Hey, Louise. You're quite the good little skater now."

"Yes, I am. I'm as fast as Tommy and Artie."

"No, you're not. Well, maybe as fast as Artie," Tommy quickly stated.

"You always think you can do what we do, and then you end up getting hurt and we get in trouble. Why don't you enjoy being as good as you are for a change and quit talking so big," I added.

"Look, I can skate in a circle and on one foot and even backwards," she said as she put on a show.

"Very impressive," Leroy said.

William and Bucky clapped for her.

"Oh, brother," I said.

"Don't encourage her," Tommy added.

"Now watch how fast I can go."

Louise took off, rounded the corner and zoomed down the hill. The truth was – she could skate fast. The thing she struggled with was slowing down and stopping.

"Shoot! We have to catch up with her," Tommy said.

"Oh, man. I was only trying to make her feel good," William said as he chased after her.

"She always feels good. She thinks she's stinking amazing. Her problem is she thinks she's too amazing and always pushes things too far," I said as we all chased after her.

We closed in fast but she had quite a lead. We knew she was likely going to hurt herself. The question was, how badly? William outdid himself. He looked like one of those Olympic speed skaters we'd seen on the newsreels at the movies – head low and focused. In no time, he caught up with Sister and literally caught her right before she crashed into a parked car. It was always a good thing to have William around.

"I think maybe it's time we got you home," he said.

Father was home from work when we arrived. He and Uncle Lyle were sitting at the kitchen table with a man I had never seen before. There was also the quirky man who lived down the street and whose name I can never bring to mind. Once in a while Mom and Dad would invite him to come over for

145

dinner and sometimes he simply showed up for dinner.

We yelled hello to everyone as we ran past to go to our room, only to be stopped by our fathers who called us back and scolded us for not giving a proper greeting.

"We're sorry we're so rude," we all apologized.

Father started, "Okay, then. I'm sure you remember Mr. Hammond from down the street."

"Yes, sir. Hello, Mr. Hammond," Tommy said and we all shook hands with him.

"And this is Mr. Thomas. I've picked him up in my cab a few times. Today he needed a ride out this way to meet with someone, but the meeting canceled at the last minute. He'll join us for dinner and bunk on the couch tonight. I'll take him back to Baltimore in the morning."

"Pleased to meet you, Mr. Thomas," we all said and shook hands with him, too.

"You children are excused until I call you for dinner," Mom said. Then she grabbed me by the shoulder and whispered to me, "My head's practically spinning and I'm exhausted from cleaning and unpacking. My goodness, the first day back and people are in and out of here like through a revolving door. You kids best behave and be quiet tonight. Honestly, it's like a circus around here."

"It's not Mom. It's nowhere near like a circus. I would know."

"I suppose you would," she said with a smile.

CHAPTER 26

Pick a Card, Any Card

After dinner Mr. Thomas pulled a deck of cards out of his jacket pocket and asked, "Would you kind folks be interested in a little magic?"

"Would we! Yes," I yelled.

He stood and held out the deck of cards in one hand and then cut them into two parts and put them back together, like Mr. Thurston had done.

"I know what that is. It's a one-handed cut," I proudly announced.

"That is correct." Then he took one card, waved it in front of us and made it disappear and reappear, also like I saw Mr. Thurston do.

"Wow! That's amazing," Tommy said.

"I know. That's the kind of thing I was trying to tell you that Mr. Thurston did," I said. "Can you do more tricks for us?"

"I think that can be arranged. But first, why don't you children make all these dishes disappear into the sink for your mothers," said Mr. Thomas.

"That would be an amazing trick," Father said.

We cleared in record time and assembled back at the table, ready to be amazed.

Mr. Thomas fanned the cards out in front of Mother. He looked into her eyes with that intense look that magicians have and commanded, "Pick a card. Show it to your family, but don't let me see it."

She chose the four of spades. He then presented the deck in front of her and said, "Place it back into the deck anywhere you like."

She placed it back into the deck and, after shuffling, he threw the deck on the table like it was a solid block of wood. All the cards remained tightly together except for one. We watched that one card flip up into the air and turn over. It was the four of spades. We went wild.

"You have to teach me that. How did you do it?" I asked.

"Young Arthur, don't you know that a magician never reveals his illusions? I've taken the Magician's Oath never to reveal the secret of any illusion to a non-magician."

He performed a few more tricks and then we kids were dismissed to go play. I didn't want to go play. This was an opportunity and I wasn't about to miss it.

"Artie, you are dismissed. Leave the kitchen and give us adults some time," Father ordered.

All the other kids went out to play hide and seek in the dark, but I waited in the living room where I could at least be close to a magician. I could hear the grown-ups in the kitchen but only like they were talking into a pillow, but that was good enough. I'd be able to tell when they were finished doing whatever they were doing and maybe, just maybe, I'd be able to talk to Mr. Thomas.

At long last I heard chairs scraping across the floor and

Uncle Lyle's voice calling out the back door for the kids to come home. Mr. Thomas walked into the living room and greeted me. "Young Arthur, what are you doing in here all by yourself?"

"I'm waiting to talk to you. I have a question. Mr. Thomas, if a magician never reveals his tricks, I mean illusions, how can there ever be any new magicians? What will happen when the last of you dies off?"

"That's a very insightful question, Arthur. The oath only applies to the common audience. It doesn't apply to the training of a new magician. There is a second part of that oath that further addresses the problem that you bring up. In a nut shell, it says that an apprentice magician must not perform his illusions until they are well practiced. That way no magician is divulging secrets to anyone who will not promise to practice sufficiently before performing. That keeps the secrets of the illusion as safe as possible."

"I think I understand. But how does somebody get to be a magician? Is there a school for it?"

"Not exactly. A magician takes on an apprentice and teaches him the art of magic. It's passed on from person to person. You have teachers and students, but not in a typical classroom. Teaching can take place anywhere. Your father tells me that you are interested in magic – that you even have plans to saw a woman in half."

"I wouldn't say I have a plan. It's more like I need a plan. I'm not using a real woman either."

"That's very wise of you, Arthur."

"Thanks. I get in enough trouble without making that kind of mistake. Tommy and I have a dress dummy. We named her Maggie. She's kind of beat up already, so we haven't gotten up the nerve to take a saw to her yet."

"Most magicians start out small and work their way up to that kind of an illusion. I like your enthusiasm, Arthur. I would even consider you a budding magician, an apprentice, if you will. I would like to teach you as the opportunity arises, but only if you are willing to take the oath never to reveal my illusions to another."

His tone of voice had such seriousness in it that it took me aback. "Not even to Tommy?" I asked.

"Not even to Tommy. Tommy wasn't the one who waited to talk to me. Tommy went outside to play. No, Tommy may possibly become a budding magician later and he may be a tremendous help to you in the future, but for now this is just for you. If Tommy begins to show promise and seriousness about the world of magic, then and only then may you have him take the oath and teach him. Are you willing to promise never to divulge the secrets of the illusions and to practice the illusions you are learning well before performing them for anyone?"

"I am."

"Congratulations. You are now an apprentice magician. Let's get started."

He showed me how to palm a card, the way magicians do when they turn their hand around and make the card disappear. He even gave me a deck of cards.

"This feels awkward and the cards feel strange."

"The slight-of-hand motions will feel awkward at first. Our fingers typically don't move in this fashion, but you'll be surprised at how quickly that awkwardness fades. As for the strange feel of the cards, magicians powder their cards to enable them to move more freely. We can't have cards getting stuck together during a show. That could ruin a good illusion. Now practice this every day, several times a day, until you're smooth. Stand in front of a mirror so you can see how well you're doing."

Then he pulled out a rope and tied it in a knot without letting go of the ends. He gave it to me to see if I could figure it out while he talked to my father. It was useless. At last he took me aside and showed me the trick to it. It was still hard to do, but I could do it. I was clumsy, but I knew I could master it if I practiced.

"Now you have a rope trick to practice and a card manipulation to practice. One more thing would be good for you as you begin. I'm going to teach you a card trick. This one you can practice for a while and then when you need an audience, try it for Tommy and your parents; because I'm not sure how often our paths are going to cross."

"Are you going to show me the one where you slam the deck down and a card flips out – like you did with my mom?"

"You're not ready for that advanced an illusion yet. Let's start small and see how you progress."

He then showed me how to have someone pick a card from the deck, remember their card and place it back into the deck with a series of moves which result in my being able to find their card. (I can't write the details of this down here. After all, I took an oath.)

"Now, I have three words for you, young Arthur – practice, practice, practice. The next time we meet I want you to be able to palm a card, tie a knot and do this card trick. Do you think you can handle that?"

"Yes, sir. Thank you, sir."

"You are quite welcome. If you do these well, I will grant you the knowledge of how to do another illusion. Before you know it, you'll be performing on stage."

"And cutting Maggie in half."

"We'll have to see about that one. For now, keep on practicing and have fun."

That night I had trouble going to sleep. All I could think about was what Mr. Thomas said – the next time he'd teach me another trick. How I hoped against hope that this was not another polite adult saying something that he'd soon forget or didn't actually mean. In any case, I promised myself right then and there that I would practice and practice those three tricks and make Mr. Thomas happy to pass more illusions along to me. I was on my way.

CHAPTER 27

There's No Place Like Home

The next morning before going down for breakfast, I stood in front of the mirror palming a card. I should say trying to palm a card. It felt weird. I kept dropping the card or I'd get it behind my hand but couldn't bring it back to the front. I realized I didn't need to look in the mirror yet. I knew I wasn't any good at this – no need to prove that in the mirror.

Tommy came back in the room and said, "Hey, if you want to eat, you better get down there. Mom's ready to give your breakfast to Sister."

"What happened to Sister's breakfast?"

"Oh, she ate it and has her eye on yours. I don't know how such a little girl can eat so much."

I slid into my chair at the table and asked Mother, "Are Dad and Mr. Thomas still here?"

"Well, good morning to you, too, Artie," Mother said.

"Sorry. Good morning, Mother."

"That's better. To answer your question, they left before the sun was up. Mr. Thomas had to get back to town."

"I thought I heard them leave, but I guess I was hoping maybe the cab would break down or something and they'd still be here."

"Well isn't that a horrible thing to wish on your father!" Mother exclaimed.

"You know what I mean. I was hoping for more time with Mr. Thomas."

"I know. He enjoyed spending time with you, too. He told me so. He thinks you've got what it takes to be a magician."

"Don't tease me, Mom. Did he say those exact words?"

"Yes, he did. Mind you, he doesn't mean tomorrow or next month or even next year, but he said you have the aptitude for it if you are serious enough to practice. Are you?"

"Yes, ma'am. I've already been practicing this morning. Oh, and thanks for not giving my breakfast to Sister."

"That girl can eat," Mother said.

"I like waking up back here in our old house," I said.

"I know what you mean. There's no place like home. I like the slower pace of things here. We're close to the city by train. There's a little grocery store a few doors down that we can walk to. School and church are here. It's nice."

"Yeah and we have a fire station right here, too."

"That's true. Thankfully we've never needed to take advantage of that."

At the corner of our street, right next to the neighborhood grocery store and across the street from the railroad tracks was the fire station. Several of the neighborhood men were volunteers, including Paul's brother Ernie. They didn't see much action; but every so often you could hear the sirens go off and watch Ernie and the other volunteers running down the street while putting on their yellow, protective coats. All along our street, doors would pop open as people tried to see if they were safe and find out what was happening.

The only time I ever saw anything was the time when lightning struck the open field by Paul's house. The fire barely got going before the guys put it out.

Ernie was the most likeable guy around. He and his wife Dolores, along with their mean dog Buttons, lived across the street in half of the Cox's house. Somehow or another they had split that big house in two – two living rooms, two kitchens, two bathrooms, two everything. Ernie's side was smaller, but plenty big enough for them and their hateful dog.

Ernie was a lot like his father. They both worked at the chemical plant in the city and they both liked children. Ernie was also a musician of sorts. He played the piano and the drums and hung around with other guys who also played instruments.

Every Saturday night Ernie and his friends went down to his basement to jam. We could hear them all the way from our house across the street. The music sounded like you were hearing it from underwater, but we knew where it was coming from.

Ernie taught Tommy to play the drums, and once in a while he would let him play with his band. Tommy made sure he was around on Saturday nights in case Ernie was inclined to let him join in.

The neighborhood kids played our usual games – marbles until it got dark and then hide and seek after dark, so that made it easy for him to be available. Tommy played with us, but he kept one ear toward the Cox's house. Paul didn't typically come outside on Saturday nights. I think her mom wanted to give her a chance to perform with the band if they would let her. Paul's mom was convinced she was raising the next Shirley Temple and was always taking her to dance or singing lessons.

But this was a strange Saturday night. Paul didn't come

outside, which wasn't surprising, but nobody from the band came to their house. The lights were out and it was quiet like a cemetery. We didn't think too much of it until the next day when Mother summoned us to the kitchen.

"Paul's sick. The doctor saw her yesterday, and he sent her to the hospital. They don't know what's going on with her yet. She has a sore throat and a fever, a bad one; and they can't get it to come down."

The hospital was a terribly scary place. We knew some kids who went there, and lots of the grown-ups who went in didn't come out. Tommy wanted to know if we could go and visit her, but that was out of the question, according to our mom.

Days passed and the Cox house was quiet. Mr. Cox continued to go to work every day and after work he would go see Pauline. Mrs. Cox, whom everyone knew was inclined to having nervous spells of some sort, was having trouble holding up. News was that Paul's fever, which had been fluctuating between 104 and 105 degrees, had come down a bit, but wouldn't budge below 103.

It was Ernie who kept us informed. Even though he wasn't allowed to go visit his own sister, he knew her condition. We didn't dare ask Mr. or Mrs. Cox anything. Mr. Cox had his hands full, and after a week of not knowing what was wrong, Mrs. Cox had taken to bed herself.

"Paul is in the children's ward," Ernie told us. "She had been lined up with the rest of the sick children, but now there is talk about her being contagious. It might even be polio; they don't know yet. So, they shoved her bed away from the rest of the children and put a tent over it to keep her from infecting anyone else."

He looked worried and tired; we were all scared for Paul. We had all had our share of mumps, measles and chickenpox, but polio was the worst fear in the childhood disease realm. With the rest of the diseases, you suffered through and waited them out. But polio was another thing all together.

Tommy said, "I'll bet she's going crazy in there."

Ernie replied, "Her fever is so high that she sleeps most of the time and doesn't have the energy to even want to do anything." Ernie's face told the story. He couldn't linger when he talked to us, he had his mom and his wife to take care of.

Day after day we would look for some signs of normalcy across the street, but there weren't any. Ernie said they didn't have any answers, and all they were doing was watching and praying. He asked us to pray, too.

I prayed a lot. I also practiced my magic a lot. There wasn't anything else going on as summer was winding down. It was so hot out even Dad didn't make us play outside. I could now watch myself palm a card in front of a mirror without wanting to throw the cards at the pitiful reflection. There was definite improvement. The rope trick was the easiest and after a week of working on it practically non-stop, I had it down. The card illusion was the trickiest. I was getting the hang of it, but my fingers didn't work like Mr. Thurston's or Mr. Thomas' did. I hoped as I grew, my fingers would get longer and work better. I diligently practiced though, like I promised I would.

Days turned to weeks. We missed Paul. We were getting more and more worried, and we were starting to think the worst.

I got up the nerve to say what we had all been thinking, "Tommy, I don't think Paul is coming home."

"What are you talking about? You don't know anything."

"It's been almost a month and all Ernie says is that they still don't know what's wrong and she still has a fever. They won't let him see her either. I'm thinking she might already be dead."

"Shut up, Artie. Ernie says her fever is lower. She'll be okay, you'll see." And with that Tommy lit into me like I'd never seen him before. He kept punching and punching until Mother came running and pulled him off me.

"Land sakes, what has gotten into you two?" she asked.

"It's my fault. I started it. Sorry, Tommy," I said. This time I truly was sorry. I wasn't just trying to get the scolding over with. Tommy seemed to be suffering enough.

For weeks, every morning we had made it a habit to look at Paul's house to see if there was anything going on there. Every morning it had been the same. The house looked lonely. The shutters and drapes were closed and no lights were on. Even Tommy was getting weary that maybe she wouldn't come home. We repeated this ritual every time we went through the living room – day or night.

Right before lunch, Tommy made a routine trip to our front window and let out a holler, "I see Mr. Cox. And Mrs. Cox."

He ran out front and was greeted by a big smile from Mrs. Cox. "We brought Pauline home," she told him. "Let's give her a chance to rest a little and you and Artie can come over later."

CHAPTER 28

At No Time Do My Fingers Leave My Hands

We threw lunch down our throats, rushed through our chores, and begged our mother to let us go see Paul.

"I think we should give her a little more time to get adjusted to being at home. She's been through a lot. You boys find something to do and you can go over around four o'clock," Mother said.

"That's long," Tommy whined.

"You've been waiting a long time. A couple more hours won't hurt you."

"I'll go practice my magic," I said. When Paul had been in the hospital a while I started to wonder if she was ever getting out of there. I decided if she got better and came home, I would put on a magic show for her. It would be my way of welcoming her home and telling her that I was glad she wasn't dead.

I had been practicing enough that I thought Mr. Thomas wouldn't mind me trying my illusions on her. I had also been practicing my banter. Mr. Thomas said it was important to use witty phrases to engage the audience. Magicians amaze and entertain, he would say.

Four o'clock arrived and Tommy and I ran across the street. Tommy pounded on the door.

"What are you doing? Don't knock so loudly. You might wake somebody up," I said.

"If they're sleeping I want them to wake up and let us in. If they're awake, then it doesn't matter."

"You like Paul, don't you?"

"What do you mean by that crack? Of course, I like her," Tommy answered.

"You know what I mean. I mean like, like you love her."

"Shut up! Why do you…"

Mrs. Cox opened the door. "Hello, boys. I thought that might be you knocking on the door. Either that or someone trying to knock it down."

"Hi, Mrs. Cox. Sorry about that. We're glad Paul is okay. Can we come in?" I asked.

Mrs. Cox hesitated, "Before I allow you to come in, you have to promise not to over stimulate Pauline."

"We promise," I said.

"What does that mean?" asked Tommy.

"It means that you are not allowed to get her too excited or stay too long. She needs rest but I think a visit from you two will do her good. Come on in."

Mrs. Cox escorted us through the living room, down the hall and up the steps, which were lined with pictures of their family. She was walking slowly; and I wondered who was more tired, her or Paul.

As much as I wanted to see Paul, I was a little afraid of what she was going to be like after being sick for so long. I didn't know if she was going to look sickly or act differently. How should we treat her?

As we stood in the doorway to Paul's room and saw her propped up in her bed, Mrs. Cox's voice interrupted my thoughts. "What this child has gone through. I can hardly believe she has been in the hospital for six weeks. Six weeks!"

Mrs. Cox pulled her handkerchief out of her apron pocket and started to cry. Tommy and I looked at her as she held her hands to her face. She began shaking. It looked like her shoulders were bouncing off of her ears. She kept sighing and saying what a terrible ordeal her poor baby had been through.

"Do something," Tommy whispered.

"What do you want me to do?"

"I don't know; you're the oldest. Maybe you should give her a hug or something. I think she's going to blow. I'll go get her a glass of water," Tommy said and he ran out of the room.

Now Mrs. Cox was sobbing and it looked like if a good breeze came through the window, it would blow her right over if I didn't hold her up. I was going to have to do something. Tommy was taking so long that I was beginning to think he ran across the street to our house for water.

"It's okay. It's okay," I said loudly enough to be heard over the sobbing. I put my hand on her shoulder to give it a pat, and she grabbed me and let loose with the waterworks. She must have been stronger than Joe Louis, especially considering the emotional state she was in. For a frail looking little lady, she had some strength. There was no way to wiggle out of her stranglehold.

Tommy finally appeared with a glass of water. "Here, Mrs. Cox, why don't you drink a little of this."

"Oh, thank you," she said as she loosened her grip on me enough for me to get free. "You're such a little gentleman. You both are."

Paul stared at us as her mother took a few sips of water. She then excused herself to lie down and recover a bit.

We looked over at Paul, who was still sitting up in bed with a sheet spread over her lap. She looked skinny and pale, but she had a huge grin on her face. As soon as her mother was out of earshot, she started giggling uncontrollably. "Hi, guys. I'm glad you could come over and see how my mom's doing."

"Are you feeling better?" I asked.

"Yes, much," she replied.

"Then shut up! Your mom's fine, strong as an ox."

We all three were laughing so hard that Mrs. Cox appeared in the doorway and cautioned us not to get Pauline riled up or we would have to leave.

Tommy and I sat on the end of her bed and she told us her story. Paul's account of her sickness was sketchy. She could barely even remember not feeling well or having a fever at home, but her mother had filled her in on the details.

She began, "After two days of a high fever, the doctor was called. He immediately told my dad that I needed to get to the hospital. Dad carried me to the car and they admitted me that afternoon. Mother sat with me, though I don't remember that. My fever evidently had hung around 104 to 105 degrees for three more days before dipping down to 103. Mom said that all I wanted to do was sleep. They had to force me to drink water."

"What was the hospital like?"

"At first I was in a big room with a lot of other sick children. The beds were all lined up. Then, after a while, they decided I might be contagious and they shoved my bed way down to the end of the room and shoved the other beds as far from me as possible. They put a net over my bed to keep me from infecting the others. Every day a nurse would come in and take blood for more tests."

"Ugh, how did they do that?" I asked.

"One of them would prick my finger and squeeze some blood out into a straw. Then my mom would hold some cotton on it until it stopped bleeding. Or sometimes they would stick a needle in my arm where it bends and draw out a lot of blood. That was the worst," she said as she showed off her bruised arms. "I could hear the nurse's cart squeaking down the hall, so I knew when they were coming. When I got to feeling better, I would pretend to be sleeping in hope that they would leave me alone, but it never worked.

"Anyway, I guess I was under the net for three weeks or so. I don't know what was going on. My brain was pretty foggy. My main memories are of the nurses and the nuns. I loved seeing the nuns come in all dressed like they do. They were quiet and sweet and never had any needles. They would talk to me and pray for me. I even talked to one of the sisters about becoming a nun. I think it would be a good thing to be."

"You'd miss playing baseball," Tommy said.

"Maybe – well one day the nurses came in with their squeaky cart. Instead of poking me with a needle, they pulled the net off from over me and gave me some tea and toast. They shoved my bed back where it had been and I could talk to the other kids. It was great from that point on. They kept me for a few days after my fever broke, to make sure that I was okay, I guess.

"One morning while I was still asleep I felt something tickle. It was my mom running her finger up and down my foot. She had the biggest smile on her face, and she said she and my dad were taking me home. And here I am, watching you two goofs take care of my mom."

"Did they ever figure out what you had?" I asked.

"Not for sure, but they are pretty certain it was polio. I can walk now though, so I don't care what it was, I'm just glad to be home."

"We're glad you're home, too. You had us scared," Tommy said.

"Scared? Scared of what?"

"Tommy thought you were going to die."

"Shut up, Artie. That's not true."

"Okay. I'm messing with you, but we were worried."

"It's alright. I heard Mom and Dad talking. They thought I might die, too. I'm glad I didn't know that. Anyway, I'm here now and feeling fine – not quite ready to play baseball though."

"Paul, I'll be right back," I said. I ran home and quickly returned with my hat, fully loaded with the cards that Mr. Thomas had given me. I stood by her bedside with my most serious magician face. I was ready to perform my first trick in public. Paul clapped as I bowed low.

"Lady and Tommy, allow me to dazzle you with a little thing I like to call magic."

I took the rope and showed it to her. "This is an ordinary rope, as you can see. There is nothing magic about it, but watch as I tie it in a knot without ever letting go of it. Impossible, you say? Watch and be amazed."

I could feel beads of sweat forming on my forehead, but I took the rope and tied it perfectly without letting go of the ends – just like Mr. Thomas had shown me.

"You will notice, at no time do my fingers leave my hands," I said with a smile.

Paul loved it. "Encore, encore," she yelled.

I took out a card and showed it to her in my outstretched hand. I flipped it back and forth, making it disappear and reappear. Paul was amazed. Tommy was amazed. I was completely amazed. I was actually putting on a show – even if it was for a very small audience.

"Encore," she demanded again.

"I do have one more thing in my bag of tricks. Take a card, any card," I said as I fanned the deck of cards in front of her.

I remembered everything Mr. Thomas had taught me. At last I was performing the trick I had practiced for so long.

"Look at your card. Memorize it and place it back into the deck."

I waved my hand over the deck and drew out the nine of clubs.

"Is this your card, madam?" I asked.

"No," she said, "It isn't."

"Of course, it isn't. Your card is the queen of diamonds," I said as I pulled it from the deck.

"I hate to tell you this, but that's not my card either," she said.

"Well, there are only 50 more to choose from. I'm sure I'll find it sooner or later."

We all burst out laughing, and I realized that was the real magic – laughter and joy. Everything was right again. Just like Paul was getting better, with time and practice, my magic would, too.

Mrs. Cox popped her head back in the room and said, "My, my, I haven't heard laughter like that in ages. It's good to hear, but I think that's enough for one day. You boys better go on home. You can see Pauline again tomorrow."

"See you tomorrow," we said. And I was happy to know that we would.

AFTERWARD

Thank you for reading my book! I hope you enjoyed your trip back to 1934. A little information for you – Artie is my dad; and Paul, the girl across the street, is my mom. (They were married from 1948 until my dad died in October 2017 after 69 years of marriage.) This book is based on Dad's stories about growing up in and around Baltimore. Many are true, some are not. Artie took on a life of his own as I wrote. Most characters are based on real family members. Tommy and Louise are Artie's real-life brother and sister.

Dad did become an accomplished magician, which gave me great pride and joy. I never lost the wonder of watching him perform. I remember him taking me to the Yogi Magic Mart when I was a kid. It was a gathering place/supermarket for magicians and is a fascinating part of Baltimore history. Dad had a career in addition to his magic, but I think magic was his first love (other than God, family, and country). He continued learning, practicing, and performing until he was close to 90 years old.

My hope is that you, the reader, will appreciate the simplicity and difficulty of life in the 1930s. There were no clothes dryers, dishwashers, or computers. Commercial airplane travel did not exist. If you had a phone in your house, you may share the line with a neighbor. People listened to the radio; television technology was just breaking through. But the same things remain important – family, dreams of the future, ambition, kindness, and God. I hope you will think about how important these things are to you.

Acknowledgments

Special thanks go to my Writers' Group, especially Rob Swanson and Leslie Santamaria. This book would not have been completed without your expertise, guidance, and friendship. Speaking of friendship, thanks to Debi Walter, my writing buddy and closest of friends, who has been by my side since Day One of this endeavor.

Thank you to my four children, Jesse, Dena, Joe, and Scott, and their spouses, Dacia, Derek, Aubyron, and Julie, for their love and support. Finally, my grandchildren, Mia, Ella, Manning, Winston, Jett, Layna, and Felix, you are the reason why I wanted to write this story. I hope you will always look for the magic.

More about Bonnie

Check out my author page at www.PrevailPress.com.

I write a humor blog at www.LifeontheLighterSide.com.

Made in the USA
Columbia, SC
27 March 2018